> Diane,
> I am so happy to have gotten to be your friend in high school. Our lives are filled with "falling stars" and their wonderful beauty. You were one in my life and my life was enriched by knowing you. Always thought you were amazing.
> Love you,
> Amy

Keeper of the Stars

Amy Lynn

2013, TWB Press
www.twbpress.com

Keeper of the Stars

Copyright © 2013 by Amy Lynn

All rights reserved. No part of this book may be reproduced or transmitted in any form or by any means, electronic or mechanical, including photocopying, recording, or by any information storage and retrieval system, without written permission of the author, except in the case of brief quotations embodied in critical articles or book reviews.

This is a work of fiction. Names, characters, places and incidences are either a product of the author's imagination or are used fictitiously. Any resemblance to any actual person, living or dead, events, or locales is entirely coincidental.

Edited by Terry & Bobette Wright

Cover Art by Terry Wright

Published by Amore Moon Publishing, an imprint of TWB Press

ISBN: 978-1-936991-65-5

Keeper of the Stars

CHAPTER ONE

'*Laura, we've decided...you need a man in your life.*'

IN RECALL, the words of her best friend rang loud in Laura's mind like the methodical clang of a death toll. Frantically she searched through the key ring in her hand, looking for the key to lock the glass door of the small boutique. Again the words clanged loud... '*Laura, we've decided...*'

Laura frowned. We've decided? There'd been a vote on the matter? When? And who voted? Donna and Rebecca? That was no vote; that was a coup d'état.

She didn't want a man back in her life. Not until *she* decided it was time.

Still the ominous toll continued without care. '*His name is Marvin and he'll be stopping by around closing time to meet you. So- be nice and smile.*'

Smile? Laura grimaced.

Not everyone had their own personal

Amy Lynn

Cupid. But she did. And while most might welcome the help of the adorable little matchmaker, she most definitely did not. Especially when that bow-wielding Cherub was in the guise of her two best friends, Donna and Rebecca.

Laura flipped through several more keys as snowflakes settled upon her long eyelashes hampering her search slightly. It seemed even Mother Nature was in play against her.

Aware her window of opportunity for escape was quickly closing, adrenaline raced through Laura's veins, fueling her movements like a full tank of high grade premium. She now had less than twenty minutes to close shop and get the hell out of Dodge. Or Denver as it was.

'He's tall, dark and handsome.'

Her hands shook uncontrollably. Whether from the cold or panic, she wasn't sure. Perhaps a little from both.

Tall, dark and handsome. Just words. Nothing to get worked up over, right? Oh contraire. In lieu of Donna's previous match-making skills, *tall, dark and handsome* meant the guy was somewhere between being attracted to the same sex and being a serial killer.

Keeper of the Stars

'I have a feeling about this one, Laura. I think Marvin could be your Mr. Right. Give it a chance. Just meet the man.' The key ring slipped from Laura's hands and dropped into the accumulating snow at her feet. Stooping, she quickly retrieved it.

Laura scowled. She wasn't ready to date again. Chance a relationship? A suffocating band of panic tightened around her chest.

It was too soon.

She'd taken a chance on Steve, her ex-husband, and it had almost cost her her life. And even if this guy she was to meet today wasn't a risk to her life, why chance her heart? Chance wasn't controllable, and in the last year since her divorce from Steve, she liked having control over things in her world. Even if it were a small world. Okay, so a very small world.

And... as for Mr. Right, she'd found out the hard way such a thing as Mr. Perfect and Mr. Right, nor Heroes and Knights in Shining Armor didn't really exist. Except perhaps in the imaginations of the heart, and Fairytales... empty wishes made on falling stars.

"Yes!" she breathed, her fingers latching onto the key she'd been so desperately seeking.

With a trembling hand Laura inserted the key. As she turned the lock she glanced up. Her reflection in the glass door stared back at her. Her green eyes appeared wide as a frightened rabbit's.

Donna would say they were yellow. Coward yellow.

Laura raised her chin. She would bear the label, only because she'd never told Donna the real truth behind her divorce from Steve. No one knew.

Dismissing her reflection, she gathered the collar of her cable knit sweater close about her throat and hurried to the only car left in the otherwise empty parking lot. Her nephew, Luke's, newly restored, midnight blue, '67 Mercury Cougar. Or, as he called it, *Sweetness*.

Laura brushed away the snow on her driver's side window with the sleeve of her sweater then slid the key into the lock and... nothing. The key refused to turn.

"No, no, no!" she whimpered softly, wishing she'd never had to borrow her nephew's car. Today her SUV was at the dealership getting last-minute maintenance before their trip to Breckenridge Ski Resort tomorrow.

Control, Laura. Yes, control. She inhaled

Keeper of the Stars

deeply feeling herself calm a bit. It helped. She remembered Luke telling her the lock system for the driver's door was acting up. The key had to be jiggled gently in the lock while turning it.

Once inside, Laura buckled up and started the engine. The car rumbled to life. The wiper blades brushed the snow from the windshield.

The unexpected loudness of her cell phone to the tune 'I Will Survive' nearly made her jump out of her skin.

She hesitated. The caller would be one of two people. Donna, a.k.a. Stupid Cupid, wanting to know if Marvin had arrived. Or Luke calling to make sure his car was still in one piece.

Chiding herself for not assigning an individual ringtone to each, she took a deep breath and pulled the phone from her purse on the seat beside her. Half in anticipation, half in dread she glanced at the caller I.D.

Donna.

Laura groaned. She'd be crazy, certifiable, to answer another call from her friend right now. She tucked the phone back into her purse.

Today she had plans. And those plans didn't include sticking around to meet Marvin, another male acquaintance, from God knows where, Donna was trying to set her up with.

Giving the car another moment for the engine to warm up, Laura extracted her tube of lip balm from her purse and tilted down the rear-view mirror. With a determined set to her lips she swathed them with the flavored balm.

Besides, she asked herself, how was she supposed to stay and face a guy whose name reminded her of the little Martian character always chasing around and trying to capture Bugs Bunny? The temptation to pretend she was munching on a carrot, wink and say "What's up Doc?" would be too great an impulse to control. And she was all about control these days.

Alas, her meeting with the little alien would have to wait until another time. Preferably-sometime well into the next century and at the end of a ten foot pole. Laura Ross controlled her own life these days. Not Cupid. And certainly not any man, human or otherwise.

As if in agreement, the idle of the car engine changed. Laura tossed the lip balm back into her purse, pressed in the clutch, dropped the gear shift into reverse and backed out of her parking space.

Keeper of the Stars

With her Marvin-*the-Martian* problem ingeniously taken care of, Laura felt a great weight lift from her shoulders. Control of her *small* world regained.

As for Donna? Laura envisioned taking 'Little Ms. Cupid's' arrows and sticking them right up her—

Crunch!

Laura's body jolted backward, then forward. The seat belt locked, preventing her from striking the steering wheel. She threw a panicked glance into the rearview mirror. The reflection of her balm covered lips parted in surprise was all she saw. She reached up and righted the mirror.

Worse!

Snow covered her back window. Snow she'd not taken time to brush off. Not that it mattered now. The sound of bending metal and breaking glass was enough to tell her she'd backed into something big. Setting the emergency brake Laura took the shifter out of gear.

Behind her car, a door slammed.

"Damn," she muttered.

She turned an uneasy glance over her right shoulder and watched the blanket of snow slide slowly down the rear window, revealing a black pickup truck. A gold Chevy emblem on the grill seemed to fill her back window. A very new Chevy emblem.

She groaned.

She didn't need this. Not now. Not tonight. She had clothes to wash, packing to do, a vacation to get ready for, and Marvin to avoid.

A knock came on her driver's window. She started and jerked around. On the other side of the glass stood a dark figure. Large and ominous, like the Grim Reaper himself.

Laura blinked, once, twice. No Grim Reaper, just a man in the typical garb of Denver's urbanized cowboy: cowboy duster and matching black cowboy hat.

Cowboy bent toward her window, angling his head against the snow blowing off the roof of her car. His turned-up collar blocked his face from view.

Not that it mattered. She didn't want to see his face, ever. A sinking feeling told her who the man was. Tall, dark and—Marvin.

Something told her he wouldn't be Martian green, nor would he have alien antennae protruding from his forehead.

Keeper of the Stars

She could well imagine how the planned mission had gone down. By ignoring Donna's call, Donna must have phoned Marvin. Red Alert, Red Alert, our subject is leaving the rendezvous area. Use any means necessary to stop her escape. I repeat, use any means necessary to stop her.

Resigning herself to the confrontation at hand, Laura unhooked her seat belt and reached for the window crank. She froze. Two words came to mind. *Serial killer.* Slowly she pulled back her hand from the window crank. "Hello," she said, raising her voice through the glass.

"Are you hurt?" His clear rich voice sounded neither angry nor upset, just concerned.

"No...I don't think so." Okay, so far he was tall, dark and had a nice voice. She released a shaky breath. "Please tell me it's just a little dent."

The man straightened, looked toward the rear of her car then leaned back down. This time his hat blocked his face from view. "Depends on what you call *little*."

The words- tiny, minuscule, and non-existent came to mind. Instead she asked, "How-how much damage did I do to your truck?"

"My truck is fine, lady, but your rear

end..."

Rear end? "No!" Laura gasped. Luke's pride and joy. *Sweetness.* Scratched. Dinged.

The announcement pushed aside thoughts of serial killers and Martians. Laura yanked on the door handle and pushed against the door. The faulty lock system delayed her for a moment but finally the door flew open.

The man stepped back quickly as Laura bounded out of the car. She was two steps to the rear of the car when she heard her driver's door shut. The lock! "No, don't..." She spun around.

In the next instant she felt her feet doing the *Curly Shuffle* on a short patch of ice. Her arms shot out in front of her then out to her sides, spinning and whirling in an attempt to catch her balance. An image flashed through her mind of her one attempt, long ago, at disco dancing. She was told it wasn't pretty.

A large hand wrapped around her upper arm, steadying her. Though the man's grip was gentle and non-threatening, the sudden contact triggered a dark memory from her past. Before her brain could register his benign intention she recoiled, throwing him off balance, too. He went down, taking her with him.

Black hole theories, parallel universe theories, even the law stating 'anything that can go wrong will go wrong', came to Laura's mind in that split second. But it was Isaac Newton's law of gravity—what stands up, must fall down, or something close, that won out.

Sucking in a breath, Laura braced herself for the impact of the fall. Impact came in the subtle scent of his cologne colliding with her senses.

The man's back hit the pavement hard, forcing a *woof* of air from his lungs.

One moment passed. Two slipped into three. Lying full on top of him, Laura remained motionless, afraid that moving, even breathing, would shatter the warm sensation strangely stirring throughout her body. Finally one thought in particular surfaced above all others. He'd sheltered her, protected her at the expense to himself. And he smelled so *damn* good.

"Are you hurt?" His mouth moved against the top of her head sending pleasant tingles down her spine. Though quite certain she wasn't injured, something had definitely happened. Not trusting her voice to speak, she shook her head.

"Good. Let's get you up and get a better

look at that rear end of yours." His voice was deep. Sexy. Filling her ear and reminding her why she had been running away...

"Ex-excuse me?" Laura gasped softly at his comment. She raised her head from its comfortable position tucked against his shoulder.

Her breath caught. *Oh-oh my!* Looking back at her, mere inches from her own, were the most gorgeous pair of gray eyes she'd ever seen.

And his flesh, not Martian green, but deeply tanned, as if the man actually spent more of his daylight hours in the outdoor elements than in a fluorescent-lit environment of an office. Beneath his hat where she had envisioned a pair of alien antenna protruding from his forehead fell a thick thatch of jet black hair.

"Your car?" he spoke, raising an eyebrow. "You wanted to check the damage to the bumper."

Warm breath blanketed her face.

Laura sought out the source of the warmth. Her gaze traveled down the bridge of a finely sculptured nose to a pair of lips that created the cutest little dimple in his right cheek when he smiled. Her stomach fluttered once. Twice.

So 'Stupid-Cupid' had finally decided to send in the heavy artillery this time. This was definitely no Marvin the Martian.

This was war.

Her brain, finally catching up, registered his words. "Bumper," Laura mumbled, feeling heat infuse her cheeks. Right, the car's rear end, not hers.

She squeezed her eyes shut hoping by some off chance a black hole *would* actually suck her in and transport her into a parallel universe far, far away. "Of course, the car," she ended weakly, opening her eyes.

His smile widened. The dimple deepened. His arms tightened about her, intensifying the warm tingles within her as he got them to their feet.

The tingles within her lingered until she caught sight of the mangled mess of metal that just moments ago had been the fender and expensively painted trunk of Luke's car. The reality of her foolishness at being in such a hurry to leave hit her hard. She brought a hand to her mouth. "This is a disaster. A catastrophe," she whispered.

Cowboy stepped up beside her. "Actually, it's not so bad." He reached out his gloved hand and plucked off a dangling piece of red taillight

Amy Lynn

lens. "Well, maybe when you get the bulbs replaced and cover the area with red tape until you order another part." He pitched the piece into the snow at their feet. "At least it's still drivable."

Laura stared down at the discarded lens piece in disbelief. "You don't understand. It's Luke's car. My nephew. I only borrowed it with the promise I would bring it back in one piece." She took in the wreckage. "He's never going to speak to me again."

"That could be a long while," responded his smooth male voice.

"You have no idea." Massaging her right temple with her fingertips, Laura thought of the hours Luke had spent in the garage working on the car. This couldn't be happening.

Quiet laughter drew her gaze up from the wreckage. Up to those eyes, his smile, that dimple—oh my!

Cowboy settled back against the front fender of his truck and crossed his arms over his chest not the least bit concerned, it seemed, of the weakened state of her knees.

"And, just how old is this nephew of yours?" he asked.

"Luke's seven..." Laura's voice trailed off

as her gaze dropped to his mouth.

"Seven? Isn't that kind of young to be driving?"

"What-no. I mean..." The provocative movement of his mouth was proving a major distraction. She took a deep breath. "Luke's seventeen."

"Seventeen." There was the suck of a short breath between a flashing row of white teeth before he shook his head and tisked.

Laura didn't have to ask what he meant. She knew. To be a seventeen-year-old male with a classic car like this put a guy in a whole different category with his peers.

Laura looked at the bumper of Cowboy's truck with its massive black vertical bumper guard. Figures. Stupid boy toys. Of course he would find humor in the situation.

She saw no humor in any of it.

A sick feeling momentarily overshadowed the fuzzies in her stomach. "Why didn't you stop when you saw me backing out of the parking space?"

"I did stop, but you kept coming."

"You could have honked or...or put your

truck in reverse."

"And if you'd cleared the snow off your back window you could be handing your nephew back the keys to his car right now."

The keys!

Biting back a sharp retort, Laura carefully returned to the driver's door of the car. She bent forward and peered through the window. Her keys hung from the ignition. Her gaze moved to the passenger seat. Her purse.

Maybe... She ran her fingertips along the top of the window. Sealed tight. *Damn!* She squeezed her eyes shut and leaned her forehead against the cold window. "No, no, nooo!" This *wasn't* happening.

There was no sound; just that scent. She opened her eyes. In the reflection of the glass she could see *him* behind her. *Oh, my.*

He leaned in close, over her shoulder, much too close. He peered into the car. Laura tried hard not to breathe, but the scent of his cologne worked its magic, slipping through the cracks of her wall of caution and control. The sensation of a thousand butterflies filled her stomach.

"My purse is in there." She sighed miserably, forcing herself to stay focused, in control.

"So it appears," he stated.

Had she heard a whisper of laughter in his voice? She turned quickly around, forcing him back a step.

"My insurance information is..." She stopped, cocked her head and listened.

Over the running engine of the car, the faint strains of *I Will Survive* resonated from the car's interior.

His expression looked pained. "Tell me you didn't actually pay for that ringtone?"

Wonderful! Mr. Right was a music critic.

"I happen to like that song," Laura stated tightly, pinning him with a withering stare. A look that should have had him scurrying back to his truck and driving away to wherever it was he came from. But he didn't.

He didn't scurry. He didn't so much as wither. He remained standing in front of her with that knee-weakening dimpled grin on his handsome face.

At six-one, perhaps six-two, she knew without slipping her hands inside his duster and running them over the whole of the man, his shoulders were broad, his chest solid, and his length, fit and lean. Tall, dark and *scrumptiously* handsome.

Not that it mattered. Not that she cared. She refused to be interested. Not now. Not ever.

Desperately needing a moment to think without the distraction of his cologne, Laura turned and carefully walked around to the passenger side of the car and tried the door handle, already knowing it would be locked. She sneaked a glanced over the roof of the car. He was watching her. She quickly averted her gaze.

What was wrong with her? She was behaving like a school girl. This wasn't control, and she needed to remain in control. Of the situation. Of herself. Control was crucial to keeping the voice of her past quiet. There was no room for error.

Reining in her thoughts, Laura leaned forward and peered through the passenger window at her keys in the ignition. Where was a coat hanger when you needed one? The thought ignited a spark of hope. Just maybe... "Would you have a Slim-Jim?"

"Wouldn't that be a parole violation?"

Criminal. Serial killer. Her head shot up. His

smile teased. Her control slipped. Her annoyance grew. She opened her mouth but couldn't bring herself to call the man standing across from her, Marvin. The name just didn't fit him. "Listen, *Cowboy*. You don't mind if I call you Cowboy, do you?"

"It works."

His smile gave her pause. Damn it, how could she be so stupid. Coming from a woman, he took the word as an endearment. No doubt an endearment he'd heard whispered into his ear countless times before by some woman lying beneath him, on a sheet-tangled bed, in the heavy shadows of night.

She clenched her jaw. "Then listen up, Cowboy. I don't do funny very well, so if you're trying to be funny, don't."

He gave her a curt nod and a poor attempt at a sobering expression. "Yes, ma'am, I'll try and remember that."

Laura doubted his sincerity. Her senses told her the comedian in him lay just beneath the surface of his next dimpled smile. Like a land mine. Ready to catch her unaware, when it could inflict the most damage.

"To answer your question, no, I don't have a Slim-Jim," he stated. "Or a criminal record," he added quickly. "Perhaps your nephew keeps a spare key hidden under the wheel well or someplace else?"

"Yes." Laura released a quiet sigh. "In his wallet."

Cowboy reached inside his breast pocket. "Here, use my cell phone."

Impressed, Laura widened her eyes. "Your cell phone unlocks car doors?" Unbelievable. She could use a phone like that. Technology!

"No," he stated slowly, fighting a grin. "It calls Luke. Have him bring you the spare key."

Laura cringed. "I'd rather not. He's going to see the damage soon enough. There's no need to rush things along." What she really wanted to tell him is she didn't want Luke's number in Cowboy's phone, giving him a way to contact her.

"Suit yourself." Cowboy dropped the phone back into his pocket. He stood for a moment before gently tapping the side of his fist against the driver's door window. "I *could* break out the driver's window. Shouldn't be too difficult. You can get the keys out of the ignition."

"What...no!" Laura gasped, horrified at the

thought of more damage. "I promised Luke I'd bring his car back in one piece."

Cowboy looked toward the rear of the car. He laughed softly. A wonderful sound that nearly buckled her knees. "I doubt a busted out window will be the first thing your nephew notices."

Refusing to retreat, Laura pressed her lips into a thin line. "Listen, if you're going to talk at all, try saying something that'll help the situation."

Cowboy stretched his forearms along the snowy roof of the car. "Let me make a call. I have roadside service—"

"As do I." Which could be almost as good as a cell phone that unlocked car doors.

"Yes, but I have the phone."

Laura glared at him.

He pushed himself away from the car and nodded toward the boutique. "Standing out here in the cold and snow catching pneumonia certainly isn't solving the problem. Let's go inside. I'm sure they'll let you use their phone to call *your* service, if you'd like."

Laura shook her head wishing it *were* that easy. "We can't go inside. The shop's closed."

Amy Lynn

"Closed? Shouldn't be." He checked his watch. "Not for another...ten minutes, at least."

"Trust me. It's locked and can't be unlocked because the keys to unlock the doors are hanging from my ignition."

The dimple appeared. "Ah. I see."

Laura was sure he didn't.

He pulled off his glove, and once more reached inside his breast pocket and extracted his cell phone. "I'll call for service. Until they arrive we can wait in my truck. You look like you could use a good warming up."

His comment evoked the image of two bodies—their bodies—in the front seat of his truck, cuddled together for warmth.

She would concede the battle with the butterflies in her stomach to his nearness. And surrender the skirmish with the weakness in her knees to his dimpled smile and... okay, maybe the short circuitry of her brain to that wonderful smelling concoction he wore, but... sitting with him in his truck?

She was at war. He was the enemy. This was a battle she couldn't chance losing.

She swallowed hard. "Call for a locksmith. Damaged or not, Luke is going to see me driving this car home tonight."

Cowboy looked at her as if *she* were suddenly the one from Mars. He shook his head. "You might be able to persuade road service to let you sit behind the wheel, but it definitely won't be to drive this car home."

"What do you mean?"

"The only place this car is going is on the flat bed of a tow truck."

"But-but you said it was drivable."

"Sure, in daylight."

Laura looked about, accessing the dimming daylight. He was right of course. She'd be pulled over and ticketed for sure if she attempted to drive home now. Or worse, without brake lights the car could get rear-ended. Still, she wasn't about to pull up in front of the house without the car.

Before she could come up with any workable plan, the car's engine sputtered once, twice, then died completely with the last of the gas. Great!

She threw him a, *don't you dare laugh*, glare over the roof of the car. His lips twitched. Not good enough. "Just call for the damned tow," she snapped.

"Listen..." He rested his forearms once again against the snowy car roof. "Let me give you a lift home. I'll explain to your nephew, man to man. You can come back tomorrow with the spare key and gas can."

Laura looked across the roof of the car into gray eyes, and it came to her. He seemed a little *too* determined to get her into his vehicle.

She could be mistaken. She'd been before.

Perhaps he really was a Martian, come to abduct her for experiments, and his truck was actually a space ship. After all, he did seem to have appeared out of nowhere.

Oh lord. Her heart pounded hard. Her mouth went dry. She was so not ready to be poked and prodded on by some alien, no matter how breathtakingly handsome he might be.

Braving what consequences may come, Laura stated with resolve, "I'm leaving on vacation tomorrow. I need the car home tonight."

CHAPTER TWO

MINUTES LATER, with the call placed to the tow company, Laura resigned herself to a long wait.

She hated waiting.

Waiting gave her time to think about how ridiculous she'd been to think of aliens, Martians, and space ships. For if he were actually an alien, she'd think he would have arrived in a silver Dodge, not a black Chevy.

Oh Heavens. She pressed her finger tips to her right temple where the slight throbbing announced the beginning of a headache. A sign that perhaps it was time for her to stop thinking.

Turning her back to the man, Laura leaned her right shoulder against his truck's fender and hugged her arms about her waist, hoping to hold in what remaining body warmth she had left.

Suddenly, his masculine voice filled her ear, and the tingle of the hairs at the back of her neck, and a chill, having nothing to do with the dropping temperature, ran the length of her spine.

"This could take a while," he said. "Let's wait inside the truck cab. It'll be warmer for you."

"I'm fine," she responded, not looking around. "Besides, you know how it is. As soon as I climb in and get warm and comfy, the tow truck will arrive, and I'll have to climb out into the cold again. You wouldn't want me to catch pneumonia, would you?"

There was a moment of silence. "Suit yourself, then," he said. Laura heard the truck door open then shut as he climbed inside.

It was for the best she had declined his offer. She didn't know him. Not at all. Still, her reaction to him had taken her by complete surprise. And therein lay danger number one.

Her marriage to Steve, The Dragon, as she'd come to call him, had been more nightmarishly hell than bliss. She'd survived and come out the other end, promising herself to be more wary. More cautious and in control.

Unfortunately, she hadn't anticipated running into Martian boy here.

Her reaction to him had taken her by complete surprise. Reminding her she was, under all her purposed control, a woman with needs.

Keeper of the Stars

And therein lay danger number two.

In such close proximity to this man within the confines of his truck she would have to guard her own actions as well as guard against his. Unnecessarily testing the limits of that control. And how well she knew that relaxing her control was certain to awaken the voice of The Dragon.

And *that* was a terror she didn't dare think about.

Restless, she glanced at her watch for what seemed the thousandth time. Only ten minutes had passed since he'd called for the tow. It might as well have been ten past eternity.

Lord, but she was freezing. Though she'd always told herself not to trust the word of a meteorologist more than any other man, this was Colorado. She should have dressed prepared.

Beneath her calf-length sued skirt, her knees knocked together like a pair of Spanish maracas. The boots she wore were more for fashion, and her sweater, though heavy, failed to provide adequate warmth.

Laura heard the truck door open behind her. Music spilled from the cab. She caught her breath. Was it her imagination or had warm air actually brushed past her cheek?

Heat *and* music? Damn.

Where the hell was that tow truck?

Suddenly annoyed that he actually chose to sit inside his truck where it was nice and toasty warm while she stood out here to freeze, Laura unfolded her arms and cupped her hands against her mouth.

The warmth of her breath brought a semblance of feeling back into her numbed fingers. She pictured her gloves where she'd left them that morning, on the kitchen counter beside the coffee pot. Lord, what she wouldn't give right now for a nice hot steaming cup to wrap her hands around.

"I have an extra jacket," Cowboy said from just behind her. "If you're not going to sit in the truck, I'd feel better if you would wear it."

Oh, I just bet you'd like me to make you feel better. "Thanks but, no thanks."

"I know you're freezing."

He knew? His assumption pricked a nerve within her. He knew nothing about her. Laura threw a glance over her shoulder then turned back. She clenched her teeth to keep them from chattering. "I'm fine."

"No you're not. Here, put this on."

Turning stiffly, she eyed the jacket. There was no doubt it would keep her warm, but she also knew it carried his scent. Butterflies danced within her stomach. She turned away. "I'd rather not."

"Okay. Then sit in my truck where it's warm."

And curl up against my chest, she could almost hear him add. He probably had a whole bottle of that magic potion cologne tucked away in his glove compartment somewhere. Her heartbeat kicked into hyper-drive. She shook her head adamantly.

He raised the jacket to her. "Don't be so stubborn, Laura. Take it."

Those gorgeous gray eyes, the scent of his cologne, his dimpled smile, his wanting to play the hero. *Oh Donna, you've definitely outdone yourself this time.* Still, Laura knew it wouldn't change her past. Nothing ever would. Hero's died, and she trusted no man. Not anymore.

Laura clenched her jaw in frustration. She was tired. No...beyond tired. She was exhausted. Enough chitchat, time to get things settled.

Amy Lynn

"Listen, Marvin, you seem like a genuinely nice guy. I know Donna had you meet me here hoping we'd hit it off, but in all honesty, I'm just not interested in dating anyone at the moment. I'm sorry she wasted your time. And I really am sorry I backed into your truck. Are you going to need my insurance information for the accident?"

He seemed to give her an odd look. He answered. "There's no damage to the truck, unless you're going to file a claim with your insurance."

Laura looked at Luke's car. If she filed a claim there'd first have to be an accident report made. She thought of her affordable premium rate. Too much hassle. She'd pay the cash to have the car repaired. "No." She shook her head. "You can go now. It was nice meeting you. Good-bye," she said, dismissing him like a game show contestant.

She watched as he surveyed the empty parking lot and its surroundings. "It's almost dark, and I wouldn't be much of a gentleman if I left you here alone. You might as well take the jacket or sit in the truck. Once the tow truck arrives and I know you're safely taken care of, I'll leave."

She should have simply told him okay and

left it at that but she couldn't. She eyed him curiously and asked, "*Are* you a gentleman?"

He smiled, the dimple teasing the corner of his mouth. "I'd like to think so."

"Even so, I'm a big girl. I'll be fine, r-really," she managed before an uncontrollable shiver possessed her.

Cowboy stepped toward her. Laura stepped back. He stopped short. "Listen, if it will make you feel safer, climb up in my truck and lock the doors. I'll wait out here. I'm from Montana. I can handle the cold."

There it was. Chivalry. With one gesture after another he was striking down her reasons for disliking him.

Her heart began to beat more strongly, as if pleading with her to take that step. To trust. Believe. The little girl inside her, who once made wishes on falling stars and believed in heroes, wanted to believe it was possible. But the woman she was today couldn't.

She'd been running away from men because guilt would never let her forget. The heart made mistakes. Memories kept her safe now.

"Have you ever seen the effects of frostbite

to the fingers and ears?" He held the jacket out to her once again.

Frostbite? She had. The word brought back disturbing mental images. It was enough. Without another word, Laura stepped forward and slipped her arms into the long sleeves of the jacket he held up for her, telling herself all the while she was only doing it because she didn't want frostbite, not because she trusted him.

The warmth of the jacket's sheepskin lining relieved her shivers immediately. The faint, woodsy scent of his cologne filled her nostrils, rebelling against her need for control. Thoughts of childhood fairytales with castles and knights in armor rushed in and pushed aside her sense of caution.

She lifted her arms to button the jacket but the sleeves were too long and covered her trembling hands.

He laughed softly. "Here, let me help." He moved in closer and raised his hands to the top button.

Caught off guard, Laura flinched at the sudden movement of his hands so near her face.

He pulled back. A slight frown creased his brow.

Feeling internally exposed, Laura averted her gaze.

Slowly, Cowboy lowered his hands. "Have you lived in Denver long?" he asked.

The sound of his voice pulled her gaze back to his, and she wished her own voice sounded as steady. "I...since birth."

"I was born here too, in Littleton, but moved away when I was eleven to live with an aunt and uncle in Montana after my mother died. Ever been to Montana?"

"No."

"That's where my ranch is. I breed and train cutting horses. Do you know anything about cutting horses?"

"Not-not really."

He nodded. "Remind me to tell you all about my ranch someday."

The smooth pitch of his voice poured over her like warm caramel on a cold Sundae. Before she realized what he'd been doing, he slipped the last wooden dowel into the buttonhole at the top of the jacket, having worked them closed from the bottom up.

"All done." He turned the collar up against

her neck. "How's that?" His gloved fingers brushed the sensitive skin below her ear.

Her breath hitched at the unexpected contact. She raised her gaze to his and knew he'd heard. The look she found there left her with no doubt. The attraction was mutual.

Suddenly there was no need for words. A pulse in the air between them became the communicator. Humming loudly, it filled her ears, blocking out all other sound. Never had she felt anything quite so powerful.

Laura allowed his gloved thumb to gently stroke the side of her face yet checked the urge to press her cheek into his palm.

His touch stirred to life hopes and desires she had never thought to feel again, leaving her with an ache that reached down into the deepest depths of her. What was happening? What was she doing? *Run*, caution pleaded, *run*.

Instead, she took a slow deep breath, filling her lungs and senses with the strong scent of leather and cologne. Danger in disguise.

In one last attempt to create distance between them she stepped back. Determined to stay on course, fighting against the emotional winds that would capsized her and drown her beneath the waters of ravenous need.

He stepped forward, seeming just as determined to close the distance she'd tried to create.

Her back encountered the truck's fender. *Trapped!* His gaze moved over her face with slow purpose, leaving her weak and breathless. Never in her life had she felt so tenderly caressed without being physically touched.

"You truly are a damsel in distress." The breath of his whisper touched her cheek with warm downy softness.

Beneath her well constructed façade of courage and control, Laura knew he spoke the truth.

Exactly how much had Donna told him? Wanting to know, she was afraid to ask. Afraid to hear him speak the answer that would break down the wall around her heart completely.

Even so in spite of her fears, Laura tilted her face, drawn to bask in the warmth of his eyes. She was sure her nose and cheeks had turned Rudolph red from the cold, but she didn't care because—Heaven help her—the look in his eyes made her feel beautiful, wanted. *Oh, God if I'm dreaming, don't let me wake.*

His thumb brushed across her lips. The rough texture of his leather glove, tugging, pulling, heightening, her sexual awareness of him. Her heart quickened.

"I-I don't need rescuing," she told him weakly.

"Your eyes tell me different."

His answer touched her soul. Laura knew they were no longer talking about her situation with the vehicles. Had he seen past the wall of ice to a heart wanting that and more? Still, rescuing would take trust, a step she was sure she wasn't ready to take yet.

"Rescuing would make you a hero," she whispered. "I stopped believing in heroes a long time ago."

"So tell me, fair maiden, what would it take to make you believe again?" he asked, the steam of their breath touching, mingling, joining. Slowly he lowered his head toward her. Her pulse raced.

'Just look at you, Laura. I can't leave you alone for a damned moment without you throwing yourself into another man's arms. Pathetic little tramp.' From within the dark recesses of her mind, Laura heard The Dragon's voice. Accusing, degrading. Her

heart clutched in panic. Steve.

The humming in her ears stopped instantly. She couldn't move, couldn't breathe. Her eyes widened with realization. Not a dream. No fairytale. No wishes come true.

Cowboy hesitated, his mouth hovering dangerously close. His warm breath blanketed her lips. Laura read the question in his eyes, and in that second she knew. The kiss wouldn't come. She wouldn't feel his mouth cover hers. There would be no rescue.

He raised his head. Gently he brushed a loose strand of hair from her cheek then, without saying a word, he turned.

A flash of loneliness burned through her as she watched him walk away.

She hadn't heard the grinding gears or the rattling tow truck pulling into the parking lot, but, he had. The dream had ended.

"Marvin, wait!" she called out.

He stopped. It felt like an eternity passed before he glanced over his shoulder. Beneath his black hat, his left eyebrow raised in question.

"Thank-you..." She swallowed hard and started again. "Thank you for staying until the tow truck arrived."

He said nothing. Laura waited, feeling as if she were teetering on the edge of a high-rise. Just when she was about to lower her gaze before his steady regard, she saw his dimple appear.

"My pleasure." He touched his finger to the brim of his hat. "And my name's not Marvin."

Laura stared at his retreating back, hoping against all hope that he would turn and come back to her. Come back and...and...*not Marvin*?

She shut her eyes and dropped her head back against his truck fender. The cold breeze a welcome respite against her heated cheeks.

Not Marvin. Deep within the long sleeves of the jacket her hands curled into fists of frustration. He truly was a stranger then. Probably a real damned cowboy even. And yet...

Laura took several deep, steady breaths to slow her wildly beating heart. What the hell just happened? With just a word, a look and a smile, he had done what no other man had been able to do. He'd put a crack in the protective castle wall around her heart.

In one foolish, unguarded moment, this stranger had her wanting to believe wishes did come true. That he was *the one*.

Laura dropped her shoulders. Her control had been tested by the storm, and she had nearly capsized. Drawing in one last deep breath, she straightened and pushed away from his truck.

***

A short while later, sitting warm in the front seat of the tow truck, contemplating on the best way to explain to Luke the damage she caused to his car, Laura's thoughts were disrupted by the high whine of spinning tires of a car pulling into the parking lot. The car fishtailed wildly before the driver gained control in time to pull parallel to the curb in front of the boutique doors.

Laura watched the driver's door fly open and the driver climb out. The man stood not far from the tow truck with his back to her. Laura's first impulse was to roll down her window and inform the gentleman the boutique was closed. But she didn't. Caution kicked in. She sat, watched, waited.

The man turned up the collar of his long dark overcoat against the cold and hurried to the boutique doors. He brought a hand up against the doors but came up short when the doors didn't open. He cupped his face against the glass a moment then slammed an open palm against the metal trim of the doors, rattling glass and metal.

Laura flinched. The violent action caused a sickening feeling to scatter the lingering butterflies in her stomach.

The man turned and eyed the tow truck. Though high in the truck's cab, Laura felt pinned by his steady stare through the windshield. She couldn't control the trembling within her.

A dark form passed beneath her window. Cowboy. Laura watched him walked toward the man who had just arrived, stopping him before the man made it any closer to the tow truck.

The two men stood, talking. Of what, Laura hadn't a clue, but every time the newcomer tried to move, step past, or look toward the tow truck, Cowboy managed to block his path or view. Finally, with a well-placed hand on the man's shoulder, Cowboy walked him back to his car where several more words were exchanged before the man climbed in his car and left.

Cowboy walked back toward the tow truck and opened the passenger door. High in the tow-cab's seat, Laura glanced down. Gray eyes looked up into hers. She welcomed the return of the butterflies in her stomach. Her gaze dropped to his mouth, looking for his dimple. He wasn't smiling.

"Who was that?" She smiled nervously, wanting to see his smile, needing to see his smile. "A disgruntled customer?"

He held her gaze. "That was Marvin. Says he was supposed to meet you at closing time, but you closed early. Running away is my guess, and I say you were right to run from that guy."

Marvin. Laura shivered inwardly recalling the man's explosive behavior. She looked back into the safe harbor of gray eyes and hoped two little words would be all she'd have to say, for him to leave it at that and ask no questions. "Thank you."

He nodded then stopped short of turning away. "Here." He pulled a business card from his pocket and penned some letters and numbers on the back of the card before handing it up to her. "I'm not doing a whole lot later tonight. Maybe you'd like to meet somewhere for a drink, coffee—"

"I can't." Laura pushed back his hand holding the card. "I've too much to do, getting ready for vacation and all. I-I can't." It was best this way.

He turned over her hand and placed the card in the center of her palm. He closed her fingers gently over the card. "Keep it anyway. For when you don't feel you have to run away anymore." Stepping back, he shut the truck door.

For several moments Laura sat, barely breathing, aware of nothing but the impression of the card against the flesh of her hand. She hadn't had to see what he wrote to know he'd penned his name and number. Her heart raced.

If she opened her hand and looked down she'd have a name to go with the flesh and blood man. But if she didn't know his name, she could pretend all that happened between them had been nothing more than a dream.

A dream would be a nice change from the nightmares she'd been having lately.

She reached up and flipped open the vanity mirror on the visor. Lord, she looked a mess. She made an attempt to fluff her bangs when her hand stilled. She focused on the scar at her eyebrow. She touched it lightly. She tilted her chin up. Her finger traced along another scar running horizontally on the underside of her chin. Both, compliments of her ex-husband, Steve. Love taps, he'd called them. *Never forget.*

Every time she looked into a mirror or closed her eyes to sleep, she never forgot.

They were the only physical signs of the deep dark secrets to her marriage to Steve. Secrets not even her best friend Donna knew about. The other damage Steve had caused was internal, within her heart. Her soul.

From the corner of her eye a movement caught her attention. Laura shifted her gaze to the figure reflected in the side mirror of the tow truck. Cowboy stood toward the rear talking with the tow truck driver as Luke's car was being loaded onto the flat bed.

For a split second, there'd been desperation in her wanting this man to be the one. Why him and never the others?

'What a sorry little soul you are, Laura.'

Laura tensed and closed her eyes against the intruding memory of Steve's hurtful barbs.

'*Poor Laura, always looking to be rescued from the evil dragon. That's what you call me, isn't it, Laura? Evil dragon?*'

Laura swallowed back the burning

sensation that flared up her throat, fighting the fear threatening to overwhelm her.

'You said it yourself, love. There are no hero's. There are no knights in shining armor. But there's me, baby, only me, and I'll never let you go.'

"Someday, Steve," Laura whispered as a tear fell to her hands folded on her lap. She stilled the movement of her thumb rubbing back and forth across the embossed surface of the business card as if it somehow possessed the magic powers of a Jeanie's lamp. "You'll see, Steve. Someday, I'll be strong enough to trust again."

Turning her face into the soft wool collar of the jacket she wore, Laura inhaled slowly, deeply. Without a doubt, the cologne was created with one purpose in mind. To play havoc on a woman's senses.

She breathed in the woodsy scent one last time. Her control slipped and her hand opened slowly with the urge to look down and read the writing on the business card stronger than she could stand. Then Laura saw him in the side mirror walking alongside the tow truck toward her door, creating turmoil with the butterflies in her stomach. She closed her hand over the card again and hurriedly brushed away any lingering trace of tears.

His stride was confident, sure. Her imagination played with the image of him on a horse with a lance, coming to fight her dragon. But then, as quickly as the image appeared, it shattered to nothingness.

She clenched her hand into a fist around the card, crushing it, crumpling it. She stuffed it into the pocket of the jacket he'd lent her then shrugged out of it. Who was she kidding? Rescued damsels in distress didn't wear sheepskin jackets and knights in shining armor didn't wear cowboy hats.

CHAPTER THREE

LAURA EASED BACK, resting her head against the large tub in the master bathroom of her townhouse in Breckenridge. Water sloshed over her breasts and over her shoulders. She sighed deeply, contentedly. Like the hot water, a sense of peace wrapped itself around her like a security blanket, just as it did every time she stayed here.

The townhome had become her haven. Bought after her divorce from Steve. There were no bad memories here.

Apart from the accident yesterday and Luke's freak-out as he watched the tow truck unload his car in the drive, she'd managed to put her vacation plans back on track.

She closed her eyes and smiled. For the next several hours Luke would be busy hitting the slopes on his snowboard. Her friends, Rebecca, Scott, and their son, Brandon, wouldn't be arriving until tomorrow. Timing was perfect for a long hot soak in the tub.

Starting tomorrow she would begin sharing the bathroom down the hall with the boys as she was relinquishing her master bedroom and bath to Rebecca and Scott for the week. But for right now, paradise in the huge garden tub was hers.

An hour later, Laura removed the tortoise shell clip from her hair. Her French braid fell like a thick velvety rope down her back, past her waist. She slipped into her full-length, terry bathrobe and tied the belt.

Thump.

The sound came from the other side of the bathroom door. She frowned and cocked her head to listen. Had Luke come back early? Concerned, she opened the door and stepped out. "Luke?"

Standing beside the bed, minus his cowboy hat and duster, was her gray-eyed cowboy from yesterday. In his hand dangled her pair of satin and lace underwear that she'd lain out on the bed with a new change of clothes.

He flashed a dimpled grin. "Hello again."

She gasped and spun around.

"Laura, wait," he called.

Once inside, Laura shut the bathroom door,

and with a resounding click of the lock she slumped against it. She pressed a hand against her racing heart, not sure what should give her more alarm. Seeing her underwear dangling on his fingertips or the fact a little part of her leapt with pleasure at seeing him again. Either, or—what in the name of heaven was he doing here? Who on earth was this guy? Had he followed her from Denver? How long had he been following her? Like a string of firecrackers lit one after the other, the questions flashed through her mind.

"Laura?"

And he knew her name. Yesterday he'd called her by her name, but that was when she thought he was Marvin and she hadn't thought anything of it.

How did he know her name?

She hadn't told him. Maybe Marvin had.

Frantically thinking to recall what personal information she might have given him, Laura began to remember bits and pieces... Breckenridge vacation, townhouse. When he buttoned the jacket for her, his voice had lulled to sleep her sense of caution. *Think, Laura, think.* What else had she told him?

Ohmigod, the accident! Had he purposely

caused the accident yesterday? How long had he been stalking her?

But why? Unable to stop them, memories from her past rushed like white water rapids through her mind, and the worst possible answer came to mind. A sickness settled in her stomach. She didn't want to think of rape, but that was definitely a possibility.

She paced her breathing and worked at calming herself. If she had learned anything from Steve, it was the brutal lesson that hysteria gave the controlling power to the other person.

Trembling, she began rummaging through the cabinet drawers and medicine chest for something to defend herself.

Q-tips, aspirin bottle, tube of toothpaste, *that's it? That's all?*

Unexpected tapping on the door made her jump.

She quickened her search. She pushed aside a toothbrush. Her hand touched and wrapped around a can of shaving cream. She returned to the toothbrush. Better than nothing.

"Hey," he called from the other side of the door. "I didn't mean to startle you."

Of course not, Laura thought. The pervert just meant to rob her of her underwear.

She held the toothbrush in a knuckle-whitening grip, feeling brave and invincible with her new found weapons in hand. If she could just make it out the door and into one of the other rooms she could call 911.

"Laura, are you okay?"

"Mister, you have two seconds to leave my house before I start screaming out the window." She shook the can of shaving cream. "And leave the underwear!"

"Mister? You didn't look at the business card I gave you yesterday, did you?"

"I-I threw it away."

He chuckled. "I'm Rebel's brother, in case you're wondering how I know you. I promise, Laura, I'm not going to hurt you."

Laura leaned her forehead against the doorjamb, needing the moment to collect herself. His voice sounded gentle, honest. Laced with a hypnotic calmness that could easily have persuaded any woman to trust him, like she *almost* had yesterday. But she was about to show him. She wasn't just any woman. She popped the lid off the shaving can with her thumb. The lid clattered on the floor.

"*Mister*, I don't know anyone named, Rebel. But I bet if I watch the nine o'clock news tonight, I'll find out which loony bin you escaped from. Now go away or I swear I'll hurt you."

He laughed.

"One."

"Honestly, Laura—"

"Two."

"Okay, but you're making a big mistake."

Laura heard his footsteps move away. She pressed her ear against the crack of the door. In the distance she heard the bedroom door shut but had no way of being certain he had actually gone out.

She waited.

And still she waited, hoping if he had remained in the room he would grow tired of waiting for her and either say something or really leave.

Her nerves grew taut with uncertainty. Deciding it was now or never to make her escape, Laura carefully unlocked the door and turned the handle. Slowly, she eased the door open a crack and listened, maybe for his heavy breathing or a creaking floorboard.

The room was quiet.

She opened the door wider. Her pounding heart pushed adrenaline through her veins. From where she stood, the room appeared empty. She eyed the phone on the nightstand.

With the can of shaving cream in one hand and the toothbrush in the other, Laura took a cautious step into the bedroom. Her gaze fell to the suitcase beside the bed. He packed a suitcase?

"They say patience is a virtue," remarked the male voice beside her.

Laura spun around just as he was unfolding his arms from across his chest and pushing himself away from the wall. He stepped toward her.

She held out the can of shaving cream. Grimacing, she pushed the button. Like silly string, a stream of mint green foam arched onto his face and hair.

"What the hell..?" He staggered back.

Laura saw it as her window of opportunity.

She bolted to his right, but he quickly stepped in front of her. Her window of opportunity closed with the rock hard wall of his chest.

He managed to wipe most of the foam from his eyes and grabbed the hand brandishing the shaving cream. The can dropped to the floor.

"Let-me-go!" she growled, trying to twist free. In her struggle, the long braid of her hair whipped around, striking him in the face.

"Hold still a minute," he snapped.

But Laura had made up her mind. She wasn't going to hold still, ever again. This time she would fight. She brought the toothbrush around like a stiletto.

He caught hold of her arm and the toothbrush fell from her grasp. "I'm not going to hurt you, I promise. Now listen to me. I'm Troy, *Rebecca's* brother."

In that second, on hearing those two names together, everything became clear. But her knee was already set in motion on its way to his groin. Troy took a quick hop back and stepped on the can of shaving cream.

Like dancers in an out-of-control ballroom spin, they twirled then tripped over the suitcase. Entwined, they fell on the bed, his weight forcing the air from her lungs.

"Get-off-me!" she gasped, twisting wildly

beneath him, desperate for freedom, feeling the memories suck her under.

He stilled, his voice sounding oddly strained against her ear. "I should first warn you though that your robe has come open."

Immediately Laura ceased her struggle.

Then, she felt it.

The heat of his body seeped through his shirt spreading warmth across her breasts.

The cold hardness of his belt buckle pressed into the soft skin of her abdomen. Rough denim jeans chaffed against the exposed flesh of her thighs.

She became aware of everything.

The sound of his breathing in her ear. The warmth of his breath against her cheeks. The sparkle of laughter surfacing from the steel gray depths of his eyes and soften like mercury when his gaze dropped to her mouth. She became aware that she was still a woman, and he was quite the man.

"Troy!" Rebecca's voice filled the room and bounced off the walls. "What on earth are you doing? *Laura?* For pity's sake. Troy, get off her!"

"Don't you *dare* move," Laura whispered in a rush, experiencing a new kind of panic.

The corners of his lips edged upward. "You're wish is my—"

"This isn't funny."

"Of course not. It's a disaster, a catastrophe." His dimple deepened.

She glared at him.

"Troy, get off her," Rebecca ordered again.

Laura felt his weight lift. Her tone changed. "Please, don't."

She turned her head toward Rebecca, just as Scott walked through the door with another suitcase. His eyes widened.

"It's not what it looks like, Rebel," Troy explained.

A moment of satisfaction filled Laura. Would serve him right to let them see him as the scoundrel he was, except it might look like she was the scoundrel's willing accomplice.

She presented Rebecca with a face she was positive had turned the reddest shade known to man. "He's right. I came out of the bathroom and… and I didn't know who he was at first. I panicked and tried to attack him. We stumbled and fell on the bed, and," She talked fast, faster than she remembered doing in a long time. "And you're not supposed to be here until tomorrow afternoon, what are you doing here now?"

"Oh." Rebecca smiled brightly. "Scott finished up with the Peterson account earlier than expected, and we were able to get away today instead of tomorrow. Great, huh?" Her smile faded slowly. "I-I left you a voice mail. Don't tell me you didn't get it?"

Consciously aware of Troy's chest pressing against her breasts, Laura tried not to breathe too deeply as she answered back. "Does it look like I got it, Rebecca?"

"I guess not."

"Well." Laura swallowed carefully. "I'd love nothing better than to lay here discussing my missed message from you, but your brother has just informed me the front of my robe has come open and—"

"Oh my!" Rebecca gasped, her hand rising swiftly to cover her mouth, which Laura suspected was more to cover a smile.

An odd silence filled the room.

"Well." Scott coughed away a laugh. He turned to Rebecca. "I'm going to finish unloading the car."

"I'll help," Rebecca added. "Come on,

Troy."

"Wait," Laura panicked. "If he gets up now…" she left the rest unsaid.

"Oh, right." Rebecca pursed her lips.

"I won't touch her," Troy said. "She'll be safe, I promise." Then he looked into Laura's eyes. "You *can* trust me."

Laura's heart clutched. There was that word again. She searched his eyes for truth.

"If he so much as takes a peek or cops a feel," Rebel warned, "I'll make him wish he hadn't."

Little consolation that is, Laura thought, but what else was there for her to do.

Rebecca moved toward the door before stopping and looking back. "I sent Troy to the boutique yesterday to pick up my order, which he left without. He should have been a gentleman and introduced himself then."

"I was, and I tried," Troy defended himself, not breaking eye contact with Laura.

"I'm sure you did." Smiling sweetly, Rebecca shut the door behind her.

Laura turned her attention to Troy, knowing anything left of her modesty was totally at his mercy. She needed distance from him, and fast. "You can let go of my hands now."

He complied, bracing both his hands on either side of her head.

"Close your eyes *tight*, then get up..." She knew she should have asked him to leave the room, but didn't. "...and turn around."

"Yes, ma'am." He nodded and winked before closing his eyes.

"No peeking."

"You're no fun," he said, pushing himself off the bed. Before he turned his back to her, Laura watched the dimple in his cheek deepen to the depth of the Grand Canyon.

"I think you peeked," she accused, quickly pulling the robe closed.

"Did not."

She sat up. Maybe he did, maybe he didn't. Still, she kept her eyes focused on a spot between his shoulder blades, ready to spring like a gazelle across the bed if he so much as flexed a muscle.

"Are you done yet?" he asked.

He sounded bored, like a small child on a car ride asking for the hundredth time, 'are we there yet'. Laura knew it was intentional, and it caused something to rise up within her to delay him a bit longer and allow herself more than a peek observation of his own person.

"Almost." She smiled, letting her gaze take a bold, leisurely stroll across his broad shoulders down his back and tapered waist and narrow hip. And farther still, down the long length of leg. Then for added measure and maybe a smidgen of spite, she moved her gaze back up to settle on the cutest, tightest male derrière in a pair of blue Wranglers she'd ever seen.

She realized the intention of her action backfired when she felt the warm pooling of desire low in her belly. Quickly, she stood and put her back to him. She tied the belt securely, knotted it once, twice. "Done." Breathing hard she turned around.

He chose that same moment to turn also. The action brought them against the other. With a feeling of déjà vu, Laura found herself once again teetering backward toward the bed.

Troy reached out quickly and wrapped his hand around her waist pulling her hard against him, crushing her breasts against his chest. Her eyes widened at the sensation. With her breathing restricted, she looked up into his face.

There was no dimple. And he wasn't laughing.

His gaze dropped to the slight gap in the robe's neckline. A drawing sensation spread through her breast and centered in her nipples. Though the robe was too thick to reveal the signs of his affect on her, she sensed he knew. His gaze rose to her mouth.

He was going to kiss her. And being kissed by this man next to her bed, wrapped in a next to nothing bathrobe, was territory that her memories forbid her from venturing into.

"I don't recall inviting *you* here," she said for need of something to say.

"You invited Rebel *and* her family."

"I did, and your point?" She hated how her voice quivered.

"Being her brother makes me *family*."

Remembering yesterday, she'd be wasting energy arguing that one. And she needed all the energy she possessed right now, for he'd moved the position of his hand, and his thumb stroked back and forth against the small of her back, producing a weakness in her knees.

"I-I thought you said I could trust you?" she reminded him.

"I did, and you can."

She should have already stepped out of his embrace, but that little thing he was doing on the small of her back seemed to be short circuiting her better judgment skills at the moment. And there was something in watching the movement of his mouth at such a close proximity that she found irresistibly fascinating.

"You wanted me to kiss you yesterday, your eyes say the same today," he said, his gaze dropping to her mouth, not at all focused on her eyes.

"I did not. And...and no they don't," she denied, yet contradicted the statement by moistening her lips with the tip of her tongue.

He arched an eyebrow. "As for yesterday, I believe we maintained eye contact for five seconds. *You* never looked away."

"And that means I wanted you to kiss me?"

"The way I see, according to my book, you look away at two seconds, that's a no. Three seconds a maybe. But five? Yeah, that's a definite, want to."

"And according to this *book* of yours, what stopped you, your reputation as a self proclaimed gentleman?"

A moment lapsed before he answered. "No, there was something else I saw in your eyes."

"What?"

"Fear."

A cold chill ran up her spine. He wasn't that good. He'd made a lucky guess. She hoped. Still, she would be wise to exercise more caution, show more control, and being in his arms like this wasn't helping. She shifted nervously, saying with false bravado, "I'm not scared of you, you know."

"I didn't say you were scared of *me*."

Laura pushed against his muscled biceps. Lightning images of naked bodies and tangled sheets flashed through her mind.

'Always willing to play the little whore, aren't you, Laura?'

She sucked in a breath as Steve's voice whispered in her head. She needed to get away, fast. She masked her turbulent thoughts behind a tight smile and quickly changed the direction of their conversation. "It would be a shame to see the hero of yesterday reduce himself to the scoundrel of today."

His eyes narrowed suspiciously. "I thought you didn't believe in heroes?"

She shrugged. "I'm thinking about giving it a second thought." She was? Of course she wasn't, she told herself. She just wanted her freedom from the Dragon.

Troy released her and stepped back. And though the desire in his eyes submerged beneath cool pools of gray, Laura found she could neither breathe nor move as his gaze boldly caressed her.

"Let me know if there's anything I can do to help make up your mind. For one week, I am at your service." His words, right words, perfect words, once more shook the wall around her heart.

A soft knock came upon the door. "Laura?"

"Rebel," Troy said with a twisted grin. "Her timing is—"

"You've still got shaving cream on you," Laura cut him off. She turned away, controlling the urge to reach up and wipe a swath of foam from his jaw. Best that he didn't confuse the trembling of her hand with desire.

"And you're not dressed."

She refused to turn and look at him. Afraid of stoking his desires again yet feeling tempted to step into the unknown. "There's a towel in the bathroom. You'd better clean up."

"Soon enough." he took a step toward her.

The door opened slowly. Rebecca poked her head inside. "Laura?"

"Rebel?" Laura quipped.

Rebecca came in with a quizzical smile. "Troy's the only one who calls me that." She walked over and looped her arm within his. "Poor guy couldn't say Rebecca when he was a little tyke, always came out sounding like Rebel. It stuck."

Laura glanced in Troy's direction before gathering her clothes off the bed. She stooped for the can of shaving cream and tossed it to him. He caught it with one hand.

"I'll meet you downstairs in a few minutes," she told Rebecca and walked out the door.

Troy's eyes remained glued to the doorway for several moments after Laura had left.

"So, what do you think?" Rebecca asked, reaching up to scoop off the shaving cream from his jaw. "Can you help her or not?"

Troy drew his brows together as the image of the gentle sensual swing of Laura's hips as she'd walked out the room shattered with Rebel's question. Yesterday he'd been on his sister's case for wanting to meddle in Laura's life.

That was yesterday, before he'd looked into Laura's eyes.

He'd been captured by the range of emotion to rise to the surface of her soft green gaze. Until one emotion in particular caught his attention. Never in his adult life had he seen such fear in a woman's eyes, especially when the woman was in *his* arms. That's when it became personal.

His gut feeling told him it would be easier riding a Brahma bull with his hands tied behind his back than it would be trying to break through Laura's wall of resistance to find the answers his sister wanted.

He had one week, starting now, to tear down that wall. Perhaps then it would be easier for Laura to step out of her shell and start dating again. *At least, that was Rebel's plan.*

Laura's decision not to date didn't bother him in the least. Especially after holding her in his arms yesterday and then again today. He liked the way she felt against him. What he *didn't* like was thinking another guy might get the chance to feel that way with her if he succeeded in what his sister asked.

He wasn't sure about the knight in shining armor bit, but Lord, what he wouldn't give to be her hero.

For one week he and Laura would be in the same house together, with nowhere for her to hide. Nowhere to run.

CHAPTER FOUR

INCESSANT TAPPING on her door pulled Laura awake.

"Hey, Laura, rise and shine, it's skiing time." Luke rapped his knuckles again.

Laura lifted her head and tried to focus on the clock. "Nooo…" She dropped back onto the pillow and pulled the comforter over her head.

She'd been asleep for two hours.

Two hours!

"Laura, are you awake?" The knob turned, and the door eased open. Luke stuck his head inside. "Hey, it's time to get up."

When she'd first taken Luke into her home, after her brother and sister-in-laws' deaths, he'd been a five-foot, nine-year-old. Now he was a six-foot-two-inch tall, seventeen-year-old. With bad manners, she suddenly decided.

Laura lowered the comforter to her chin and scowled. "I heard you the first time."

"Jeeze, you don't have to bite my head off."

Luke pulled his head back and shut the door, grumbling something about grumpy old people.

Moaning again, Laura threw back the covers and climbed out of bed. She snatched up her robe. She pulled her braided hair over her shoulder, glad she'd left it that way. She didn't think she could have mustered the energy to re-braid it now.

A shower. That's what she needed to kick-start her morning. That and a large cup of coffee. Black, non-decaf, something strong enough a spoon could stand up in.

Taking a tentative step out into the hall, she glanced toward the other bedrooms, the one next to her own in particular. Only Luke's door down the hall stood open. If luck were on her side, Troy would still be asleep, and she could take her time in the bathroom, now that she had to share the one down the hall. She spied the bathroom door partially open and approached it on tiptoe.

Another door down the hall behind her opened. Not yet ready to face Troy this morning, panic struck. With a speed that might have won her an Olympic gold medal, she sprinted to the bathroom, slipped inside, closed and locked the door.

She'd made it.

She closed her eyes and turned around. Leaning back against the door she pressed a hand against her racing heart and released a huge sigh of relief.

"Well, good morning, sunshine!"

Her eyes flew open.

Troy's shirtless reflection greeted her. He stood in front of the mirror that ran the length of the double sink counter, just wiping the last traces of shaving cream from his freshly-shaven face. His hair was still damp and uncombed. A white tee shirt lay on the counter beside him.

"Sorry," she breathed. She had never considered the bathroom small. But now, with him, his reflection and her, not to mention the added arrival of butterflies in her stomach, it wasn't nearly big enough.

"I didn't realize you were in here." She turned quickly and unlocked the door, annoyed with how easily the simple sound of his voice could knock her off balance. Strip her of control. "You really should learn to lock the door." She opened the door to leave.

"Or, you could learn to knock."

She halted her exit, yet refused to face him. "I'm not playing this game with you. Let me know when you're through."

"Wait," he said. "You can stay. I'm finished."

Against better judgment, she glanced over her shoulder, catching his reflection in the mirror. Laughter gleamed in his eyes.

He reached for his tee-shirt. The movement drew her gaze away from his eyes. His skin, smooth and tanned, resembled finely finished oak. His chest conjured up fairytale images of a knight's breastplate of armor, honed to perfection, his nipples, small and hard.

Her gaze dropped lower still to the muscled six-pack of his abdomen. She knew she should have stopped there, but something inside her rebelled, refusing to obey. Screamed for freedom. *Okay, Laura, get hold of yourself. He may look flawless, but then so did Steve.*

Still lower, he'd left the top button of his Wranglers unbuttoned and her eyes followed the thin trail of black hair that ran below his navel and disappeared behind the waistband of his black boxers.

In spite of wanting to find one physical

flaw, she had to admit, she couldn't.

He slipped his forearms through the tee-shirt and raised it over his head. Each movement orchestrated a symphony of flesh and muscle, triggering an unchecked yearning to feel their strength wrapped around her, protecting her, gently holding her.

Breathless, she made herself look away yet felt something stronger drawing her gaze back. He was magnificent. *Could then the flaw be internal, with his character, like Steve's had?*

Finally, he tucked in his shirt. Laura watched his fingers work the last button on his jeans closed before she looked up into the mirror. He was looking back. A spark of bedevilment danced in his gray eyes.

Embarrassment heated her cheeks. She'd been caught watching. Under the sink cabinet would be a good place to hide right about now, she thought.

He picked up his razor and a can of shaving cream. "It's all yours, sweetheart." He paused, raising an eyebrow. "Unless you need me to stay and help."

As if. "In your dreams, mister."

He turned and parked himself against the sink counter, crossing his legs at the ankles, looking to be in no hurry to leave. The corners of his lips edged upward. "Maybe if you're going to take a shower, I could stay and help with the hard-to-reach places."

"Not in your *wildest* dreams."

"My, my." He clicked his tongue. "Did we get up on the wrong side of the bed this morning? Or could it be we didn't get enough sleep last night?"

"Don't you have a cow to milk or a field to plow somewhere?"

His deep sexy laugh filled her ears. "I'm a horse breeder, not a farmer. There's a difference, remember?"

She shifted her weight to her left foot, refusing to give in and smile. "Are you done in here or not?"

For a moment he remained silent. That couldn't be good. "Well?" she huffed. "Are you or not? It's a question that requires a simple yes or no answer."

"Do you ever leave your hair unbraided?"

The question stopped her. "Never."

"Too bad. I bet it's something to see. Maybe

I'll have to make it a wish."

Laura shrugged. "You can wish for the moon, if you like."

"I think I'd have better luck on a star."

A chill rippled up her neck.

"A falling star," he added.

Laura felt her chest constrict. "You'd have to see one first. And it's not like you can just look up and see one in the sky on command, you know. You could end up watching night after night, for weeks on end or even—"

"I saw one last night. Actually, it shot more than fell." He raised his hand, letting it arc then drop.

The remark took her thoughts back to last night. To the shooting star she had wished upon before falling asleep.

In the darkness of her room, she'd stood by her window and raised her hand high, cupping it against the cold pane of glass. The stars, twinkling like millions of diamonds on an unraveled bolt of black velvet, had seduced her thoughts into remembering a rhyme her grandmother had taught her long ago.

Maker, keeper of the stars, release for me one

Amy Lynn

wishing star. Followed by a tail of light, to shine upon my hearts delight.

Seconds had passed by. Nothing.

She sighed wistfully. It'd just been a silly old rhyme anyway. So she'd spread her fingers against the window, releasing her imaginary handful of stars. But as she did, one bright star shot out, blazing an arc across the night sky.

She'd closed her eyes, and with no time to think, made her wish. *A love to come and right the wrong, a knight in shining armor strong.*

And now this morning here they stood, talking about falling stars. Goosebumps rose to the surface of her arms. The blood rushed to her head. "You...saw a falling star...last night?" Her voice came out sounding small.

"Actually," he corrected, "very early this morning."

Her head pounded.

He said, "I had a hard time getting to sleep last night, sat for some time looking out the window at the stars, thinking about my place in Montana."

Laura turned. Her movements became mechanical. She pulled open the cabinet drawer with a trembling hand. "You can tell me about your insomnia some other time. Right now I'd like to use the bathroom, *alone*, please." She pulled out her toothbrush and toothpaste, doing something, any kind of movement, to give her mind some distraction.

He pushed himself away from the counter. "Arming yourself again?"

In spite of herself Laura smiled. "What do you think?" She knew he was remembering their tussle the night before.

Taking a step toward her, he gave the can of shaving cream a quick shake. "I think it's payback time."

"You wouldn't dare!" she gasped. But even as she said it, she knew he was just ornery enough to do it. She took a wary step backward. Sometimes, running away was the best thing to do.

Her heel bumped the door, and she heard it click shut behind her. Then again, if escape wasn't an option...

She held up the toothbrush. "What? You didn't get enough last night?"

His laugh wasn't what she expected. Flipping the can in his hand he held it out to her.

"Take your best shot, darlin'."

From behind her came a light tapping on the door. "Ah-hem." Rebecca cleared her throat. "Are you two almost done in there?"

Laura's gaze flew to Troy's face. "Now look what you've done," she whispered heatedly. "After last night I can just imagine what she's thinking."

"Oh, it gets even better, honey." The dimple in his cheek took on the depth of a small crater. He set the can of shaving cream on the counter then raked his hands through his hair, giving it a sexy, played with appearance.

He cleared his throat, loudly. "Ah, yeah...give us another minute, sis."
"Get out, now!" Laura turned and jerked open the door, giving Rebecca, still standing on the other side, a start. "And for your information, *cowboy*," she said as he stepped past her and into the hall to join a confused Rebecca. "That falling star was meant for me last night, not you!" And with that she forcefully closed the door behind him.

CHAPTER FIVE

LAURA'S SKIS FURROWED through a new layer of white powder. The combination of cold mountain air and the thrill of skiing had knocked out the last dredges of fatigue and kicked in a rush of adrenaline.

She didn't mind that the others had headed off to the more advanced slopes. Her skill topped out on the intermediate run. Pushing herself raised the chance of losing control. And for her, control meant everything.

She maneuvered around a small island of pines. Sunshine flickered like an old time movie reel through needled branches, reflecting off ice crystals.

Her surroundings sparkled and glimmered. It was easy to imagine herself gliding through a fairytale world.

Perhaps she was in her element in the cold and snow. So what if the men that Donna had sent her way had nicknamed her, Ice Princess, coldhearted when it came to love.

Let them make jokes. Let them talk behind her back. They were lucky to have walked away with just a touch of frostbite.

She frowned as another thought came to mind. Now she had cause to worry. One man now seemed more prepared and determined to weather the cold.

If she were the Ice Princess, then surely Troy was the Prince of Fire. He was dangerous. Dangerous the way a wildfire consumed everything in its path. And he seemed to have set a course straight toward her.

Laura approached the end of the run and turned again toward the lift line.

"Laura!" The familiar voice shattered her reflective mood.

Speaking of the pyromaniac.

She checked her place in line. Two chairs separated her from catching a ride up the mountain. She wouldn't make it before he reached her.

Troy skied up beside her.

"I'm skiing, go away." She moved up in line.

He followed. "Perfect, I'll go with you."

She looked at him.

His dimple, like the strike of a match, appeared right on cue.

The chair came around and scooped them into the air. Her resolve to ignore him lasted all of two seconds.

She chanced a glance at him out the corner of her eye. Settled back with his arms crossed over his chest, his eyes could have been closed behind his mirrored glasses, but she couldn't be sure. He seemed in no hurry to talk to her, and if he thought she would begin, he was in for a long, cold wait.

Approaching the quarter point, the wheel turning the cable slowed to a stop, setting the chairs rocking. Laura looked over her shoulder. The two chairs behind them were empty. She couldn't see the cause for this delay.

She glanced at Troy.

He hadn't moved. By all appearances he could have been asleep.

She fidgeted. The silence suddenly unbearable, she gave in and spoke first. "What do you think happened?"

He raised his shades and opened one eye to

look at her. "I tipped the operator a hundred to stop the lift after we got started."

Laura spotted the slight twitch to his lips and rolled her eyes. "You're so full of—"

"Crap?" he finished, unveiling a full grin. He lowered his shades back into place.

She watched a breeze ruffled a thatch of black hair against his forehead. "Why would you do that?"

"So we can finish our conversation from this morning."

"About what?"

"Our falling star."

"You mean *my* star?"

"What did you wish for?"

Laura stared at her distorted image in the lenses of his shades. That's how it would have to be with him, light and with a teasing air. Anything deeper would risk exposing her vulnerability.

She leaned close and whispered. "If I tell you, I'll have to kill you."

A grin split his face and he laughed. The rich sound filled her with warmth.

"That could prove exciting. And how would you go about doing such a dastardly deed? By killing me with kindness? Or better yet. If you wanted to watch me die slowly, you could always try loving me to death."

"Stop it." Light banter wasn't working after all.

"Stop what?"

"Taking everything I say and turning it into something—"

"Sexual?" he finished.

"Ohhh!" She wanted to shake him. They were fire and ice. "Quit finishing my sentences. I find it highly annoying."

"Okay, I'll behave."

She slanted him a doubtful look.

His expression turned to one so much like a little boy wanting to make amends. His smile became infectious.

He touched her hand. "Now that's a smile from the heart if I ever saw one." His voice softened. "That's all I've been trying to get you to do. Smiles look good on you."

Laura opened her mouth to respond when the sound of an angry voice carried gruffly in the air. She felt herself turn cold inside. She'd lived with a man who, in the privacy of their bedroom, used the same tone as the man in the chair ahead of them.

"You worthless whore!" the man yelled at the woman beside him. When he put a wineskin to his mouth and tipped his head back, Laura guessed he was drinking more than water.

The familiarity of the verbal attack and the low desperate pleading of the woman beside him caused Laura to shift uncomfortably. A cold foreboding iced its way up her spine.

"Sounds like he's had one too many," Troy stated quietly.

Laura glanced at him. "That doesn't excuse his behavior."

"I wasn't making excuses for him." His brows dipped in a frown.

"You look at another man again, I'll beat the crap outa ya," the angry man shouted. "Do you hear me, bitch!" The man leaned over and snarled in the woman's face.

"He's gonna hit her, Troy." Laura knew the pattern well.

Troy looked at the cable overhead then over the sides of the chair before his focus turned to the couple ahead. Laura watched him make a fist, opening and closing it against his thigh. Oddly, his concern helped soothe much of her fears.

"Stupid little slut," the man said.

The woman tucked her head into the collar of her jacket. Laura knew what she was feeling, all too well, and her heart went out to this woman, this stranger, this fellow victim of abuse.

Like a whipped child, the woman chanced a peek over her shoulder to see who had witnessed her verbal abuse. She made eye contact with Laura, and Laura tried with all her mental energy to transfer some of the strength and understanding to the woman.

The man turned too but mistook who the woman beside him had looked at. He glared at Troy. In slow-motion horror, Laura watched the man turn to the woman and grab a handful of hair.

Hearing the woman's quiet, controlled grunt of pain, Laura flinched, reliving her own memories.

"Why, you dumb, stupid, little slut. I warned you, didn't I?" He jerked the woman's head back. "Now it's your fault."

Laura gasped.

"Son-of-a-bitch," Troy growled. The muscle at the back of his cheek flexed rapidly.

Amy Lynn

The cable overhead made a noise. The line of chairs swung into motion.

"Hey, buddy," Troy called out.

The man turned his bony face around. "Yeah, what the hell do you want?"

"How about taking it easy?" Troy urged lightly. "We're all out here to have fun."

"How about taking this?" The man laughed harshly before giving Troy the finger, followed by the verbal definition of the gesture. The man turned to the woman beside him. "You wanna screw him too?" He smacked the back of her head, jerking it forward with the force of the assault.

"Ohmigod!" Laura's hand covered her mouth in horror. Her other hand grappled for the sleeve of Troy's jacket.

Troy reached up and covered her hand with his, squeezing it gently as if to reassure her. Once again the lift came to an unexpected halt. The situation looked to be getting worse.

"Hey, buddy," Troy called out to the man again. "Real men treat their women better."

"You think you're such a big man, bring it on. I'll knock the crap out of you too," the man yelled back, showing Troy a fist.

"What- what are you doing?" Laura stared

wide-eyed at Troy.

"I'm thinking maybe if I can redirect his anger, he'll leave the woman alone."

"You'd take that risk? What if he pulverizes you once we get off the lift?" Concern for his safety welled up inside her.

"Sometimes you have to take the risk." He removed his shades and winked at her. "Don't worry, I can handle him once we get our feet on the ground."

The lift started again. As they passed through a group of trees, the wheelhouse came into view though still some distance away. Laura turned her attention to the commotion in the chair ahead. The man placed his hand on the woman's back and gave her a quick shove. The woman reached out, trying to hold onto the side bar, without success. She fell like a discarded rag doll to the ground below.

Like shattered glass, Laura's scream pierced through the air. Troy's head shot up.

The man sat alone, glancing over the back of the rail to the ground below. The woman's body appeared broken and lifeless.

Someone several chairs behind them

shrieked, "Call 911"

"Ohmigod. Is she dead?" another rider cried out.

Troy turned to Laura. "There's no time to wait. I have to see how bad she's hurt." He placed his hand on Laura's. "Listen very carefully and do exactly as I say."

Laura's heart pounded hard in her chest. She nodded, her hands trembling with shock. He had to feel it.

"If he," Troy emphasized who, with a jerk of his head, "gets off the lift, stay on. Whatever you do, *don't* get off." He touched her cheek with a gloved finger. "Ride to the bottom and wait for me. Will you do that?"

He was asking her again to trust him, to have faith in his actions. She knew he was going to take the twenty-foot jump to the snow below. The plan was crazy, but she agreed.

He released her hands and moved to the edge of the chair. Then, putting his gloved palm against his lips, he blew her a kiss. "I'll see you at the bottom." Then, he jumped.

A commotion rose up from the passengers behind her. She ignored their cries of alarm and focused her attention on Troy. He hit the deep powdery snow and managed to stay upright on his skis.

Laura slid over to the spot he'd vacated to better observe the rescue. He looked up to her before pushing off toward the motionless woman. Laura held her breath.

Troy knelt beside the woman. An eternity passed before Laura saw him raise his head. He smiled, giving her a thumbs-up.

Laura released a pent up breath and turned around. She found herself looking at a distance into the eyes of the man on the lift in front of her.

He'd turned around and draped his arms over the back of his chair. He gave her the eye. "Hey, honey, looks like your hero boyfriend's gone and left you all by your lonesome. Wha'daya say you and I spend a little quality time together?"

Stay on the lift, don't get off. Troy's voice echoed in her head. Now she understood why. She shuddered. Still, if the man knew she was staying on, he might do the same. She had to make him think she was getting off, too. She forced a friendly smile and edged forward as if ready to slide off the chair.

When the chair rounded the wheel he was

there, waiting for her. She let her skis skim the surface of the snow. He moved toward her unsteady and unbalanced.

Her chest hurt from the force of her pounding heart. She eased off the seat, letting it push her along. Then at the last possible heart stopping moment she hopped back on. The chair whipped around and headed back down the hill.

She was on her way to safety.

The man spewed out a string of curses. She looked back and watched him push off on his skis. She relaxed. She was safe. The authorities would be at the bottom if he decided to follow her.

Her gaze ran a path from the man to where Troy knelt with the woman. But then shot back to the man, as it suddenly dawned on her that he had turned his skis down the slope in Troy's direction.

Alarm seized her heart. Troy seemed unaware of the danger accelerating down the slope toward him. His attention focused solely on the woman in the snow.

"Troy!" Laura's voice echoed against the mountainside.

He looked up.

He had no more time to stand and move several feet away from the woman before the man slammed into him, the impact sending both men tumbling down the mountainside. Laura could do nothing but watch helplessly.

And the chair carried her away.

Amy Lynn

CHAPTER SIX

LAURA FLIPPED through the pages of a magazine, but her thoughts were elsewhere. When she reached the last page she turned back to the beginning and started over again.

She sat beside Scott and the boys in the emergency room while Rebecca had gone back with Troy to the attending area.

She got to the last page in the magazine, stopped and turned back one. The article was about meteor showers. A small picture in the top left corner of the page showed a shooting star.

'What would it take to believe again?' Troy had asked her the day she'd backed Luke's car into his truck.

Once there was a time when she did believe....

'How many falling stars will we see tonight, grandmother?' seven-year-old Laura leaned close and whispered.

'Maybe two, one for me and one for you.'

Keeper of the Stars

Sitting together in the dark, Laura and her grandmother looked out the bedroom window at millions of stars blanketing the heavens.

'How does the rhyme go again, grandmother?'

Slowly grandmother began. 'Maker, Keeper of the stars, release for me one wishing star. Followed by a tail of light, to shine upon my hearts delight.'

They watched. They waited. Then Laura finally asked, 'But what if we see only one?'

Grandmother tucked a strand of hair behind Laura's ear. 'Then you can make the wish.'

'Don't you have any wishes?'

'You and your brother, Jeffery are my wishes come true.'

Laura frowned. 'I'm going to wish Jeffery into a warty ole' toad.'

'Laura Ann, what would make you wish for such a thing?'

Laura turned her frown toward the stars in the sky. 'Cause he chases me with ugly ole' bugs, hides my Princess Tina doll and...and he hits me. I don't like it when he hits me.'

'No,' grandmother said. 'It isn't nice for boys to hit girls.'

Laura brightened. 'Instead of wishing Jeffery

into a warty ole' toad, can I wish for someone bigger to sock him in the nose?'

Grandmother hid her smile. 'I have a much better idea, Laura. How about we wish for a boy to come along who'll treat you real nice. Would that do?'

Laura made a face. 'But I don't want a stupid ole' boyfriend.'

Grandmother wrapped her arms around Laura's shoulder and pulled her close. 'Someday you will. And he'll be handsome, strong and courageous and treat you like the wonderful princess you are.'

'Grandmother, look!' Laura pointed toward the heavens. 'Make the wish for me. Hurry, grandmother, hurry!'

Grandmother snuggled her tighter and said, 'I wish a love to right the wrong. A knight in shining armor strong.'

"Troy will be okay, he's pretty tough." Scott placed a consoling hand on Laura's forearm, bringing her thoughts back to the present and a halt to her mindless page turning.

"I know he will." Still, she continued glancing anxiously toward the door.

She'd been channeling all her energy in keeping the thin thread of composure from snapping completely in two. The events of today, on top of her lack of sleep the night before, were taking their toll. The last thing she needed was to lose control and break down in front of everyone.

A nurse pushed through the door.

Laura sat up, but the nurse looked past her and motioned to a woman at the back of the waiting room. Laura blew out a deep breath and turned to Scott. "I know he'll be all right, but the collision looked so awful. I felt so helpless on the lift."

"There wasn't anything you could have done. Just be glad the ski patrol was able to get to that poor woman as fast as they did."

"You're right," she agreed and glanced back at the magazine.

The fall from the chair had broken both the woman's legs and her pelvic bone, but that was the worst of it. At least physically. Emotionally, Laura knew it would be an even longer road of recovery, a road she was still traveling herself.

Laura fanned through the magazine but stopped when an ice cream ad caught her attention. *Pralines and cream.* The last time she'd eaten pralines and cream was the night she was in the emergency room. The night Bobby had tried to rescue her from Steve.

The memory erupted from its deep dark hiding place like a volcanic explosion, and with it Laura felt its lava hot pain all over again.

Luke's fifteenth birthday, but she'd sent him next door that night because Steve had lapsed into one of his *moods*. They'd argued, Steve and her.

About what? Yes, she remembered now. They'd been at a stop light. A man in the car beside them looked at her and smiled. When they'd got home Steve accused her of flirting. Always flirting, always wanting to play the whore, he'd said.

He'd hit her then. His fist split open the underside of her chin. The impact of her head striking the dresser had opened a gash at her eyebrow. He'd hauled her up by her long unbraided hair and slammed her against the doorframe. He was about to do it a second time when the doorbell rang. It had been Bobby, bringing Luke a birthday gift. He hadn't known Luke wasn't there. Oh, God, he hadn't known.

Between running and stumbling down the hallway she'd managed to get to the front door before Steve could send whoever it was away.

Keeper of the Stars

Before he could lock the door and finish teaching her a lesson. Still, Steve was right behind her, reaching out for her when she'd yanked open the door.

Ugly, everything turned so ugly and got even worse.

"Son-of-a-bitch." Bobby had said when she'd fallen into his arms and he'd seen her face. "Get in the car, Laura. I'm taking you to the hospital." Then he'd shielded her, stepping in between her and Steve.

"Get your filthy rotten hands off my property, you wife stealing bastard," Steve had yelled. "Laura, if you know what's good for you, you'll get back in the house right this instant."

Bobby had grabbed Steve's shirt front, slammed and pinned him against the doorframe. "You worthless piece of shit. So help me if I ever find out you've used her as a punching bag again, God as my witness, I'll come back and I'll kill you."

She'd climbed into Bobby's car while Steve stood on the doorstep screaming accusation of adultery at them both. Slut, whore, Steve's pet names for her echoed up and down the street as

Bobby backed his car out of the drive.

On the way to the hospital it had begun to rain, hard.

"I know him, Bobby, he's not going to let me go," she'd told him.

"I was your brother's best friend. I've watched over you since we were kids, Laura, and just because you're married does it mean I'm going to stop now. Besides, I promised your brother before he died..."

"You'll always be my hero, Bobby," she'd managed telling him through her injuries.

"Ah, hell, Laura, I'm no hero, I'm just your best friend. What you need is a knight in shining armor to come along and slay that damned dragon you married."

Then they were hydroplaning. The car spinning, spinning, it seemed a hundred times before it impacted the concrete barrier. Then darkness.

When she awoke in the emergency room, Steve was beside her. Bobby was dead.

Apart from the damage done to her before the accident, her injuries were minor. Steve took her home. He was calm and remorseful, of course. He spoon-fed her ice cream. Her favorite. Pralines and cream. Then slowly, carefully he carried her to their bedroom where he had sex with her, to show her how sorry he was about losing his temper.

That was the last time she ever ate pralines and cream. And the last time she ever allowed herself to believe she could be rescued. Steve never hit her again, but he seemed to take his delight in verbally abusing her. Always accusing her of having affairs, cheating, whoring around.

Bobby had been her best friend, her hero, but never her lover. Heroes were the ones who died to save us. She didn't need a hero right now. She didn't want anyone else risking their life to save her. What she needed was as Bobby had said. Only this time, a knight in shining armor to ride in and slay the memory of the dragon first.

The loud swish of the emergency door opening pulled Laura's thoughts back to the present. Rebecca appeared. Laura's heart leapt. She and Scott stood, but she held herself back, letting Scott speak first.

"Well, what're the damages?" he inquired, enveloping his wife in his arms as she walked up to him.

Rebecca shook her head. "He took a hard

hit."

"Skiing isn't intended to be a contact sport." Scott smoothed his wife's hair.

"He has a dislocated shoulder, a hairline fracture to his left wrist and some bruised ribs." Rebecca recited the doctor's diagnosis.

"It's bad, but I suppose it could have been worse." Scott kissed his wife's forehead.

"And a possible concussion," Rebecca added. She touched Laura's arm. "He wants to see you."

"Me?" The butterflies stirred in her stomach.

"He said something about a conversation the two of you didn't get to finish."

Moments later, Laura tentatively pulled aside the curtain around the cubicle the nurse had indicated Troy was in. The light above the bed was off. Laura stepped inside, letting the curtain fall closed behind her, then moved to stand by the bedside chair.

Troy's eyes were closed. His right arm was cradled in a sling, with his wrist, up to his forearm, freshly cast. Sprouting from the white plaster, like some science experiment gone bad, his fingers protruded, swollen and discolored.

Though he was shirtless, his upper abdomen had been bound with bandages to restrict movement of his ribs. A white hospital blanket had been draped over his legs and hips, but she could still see the elastic waistband of his black boxer shorts.

With a twinge of guilt, Laura glanced away. He was injured and bandaged and she couldn't help thinking, even so, he was still a fine specimen of a man.

'Wake him up.' She remembered the nurse's words and reached out a hand to wake him, his name ready on her lips. But an unexplained boldness came over her. Instead of touching his shoulder to wake him, her hand reached out toward his hair. It felt soft like black velvet, teasing the sensitive skin between her fingers as she raked them through the thick mass.

Her gaze took a leisurely stroll down his forehead until she stumbled into a pair of half open gray eyes. She snatched back her hand.

"That felt nice," he whispered.

"I-I thought you were asleep."

"Not with this headache." He opened his eyes fully, absent the devil may care sparkle she had become familiar with. Though his eyes were clouded with pain, something broke through the surface and tugged gently on her emotions.

He brought a hand up, but she stepped back before he could touch her cheek with his fingertips. His hand dropped back onto the bed.

"I made my statement to the police," Laura said.

"I've asked about the woman but can't seem to get an answer."

"They say she's going to be okay."

He lifted his cast wrist, his smile failing to brighten his eyes. "So much for trying to play hero."

A surge of unexpected warmth filled Laura's chest, for she found no trace of self-pity in his tone, just a frustration that he couldn't have done more. "You did just fine. Kinda reminded me of Tom Cruise in a *Mission Impossible* movie."

"Tom Cruise, huh?" He took a slow painful breath and grinned unconvincingly. "I hear he always gets the girl in the end."

He pressed his good hand onto the mattress in an attempt to sit up straighter. He grunted and placed his hand over the wrapping at his side.

Concerned, Laura stepped forward.

"Should I call the nurse?" She covered his hand with hers, unsure of how to help.

"No. Just hurts like hell is all." He turned his hand so that he held hers and shot her a pained glance. "Here I was, worried it was the jump from the chair that would kill me." He raised an eyebrow. "Your wish on that star...it didn't have anything to do with wanting to see me drop off the face of the earth, did it?"

She opened her mouth, but before she could respond, the curtain moved aside, and a tall brunette in a long white smock walked in. Laura attempted to pull her hand away, but Troy curled his fingers around hers and held it against him.

The doctor checked papers on a clipboard. She raised her head and looked at Troy. "Well, Mr. Hawke, along with your other injuries, you have a mild concussion."

She reached out toward Laura. "Hi, I'm Dr. Payne." She laughed at Laura's expression. "I know, the name is a bit of an irony for my profession, but it makes for a great icebreaker." She shook Laura's hand before sitting on the stool beside the bed. "Your husband is a very lucky man, Mrs. Hawke."

Husband! Laura opened and closed her mouth like a fish out of water. She looked at Troy for help, but his face was twisted in a painful grimace as if fighting back a laugh.

Her frame of mind was too fragile at the moment to play silly games. "I'm not his wife," she explained.

"That didn't keep us from sharing the same bathroom this morning," Troy said, giving her a teasing wink.

The doctor looked up, her expression one of amused interest.

Laura threw Troy a glance, her eyes narrowed in warning. "What I mean is—"

"What Laura is actually trying to say, is we're both lucky. To have each other, that is." He looked up. "Isn't that right, *muffin cakes*?"

To her further unnerving, he raised her hand to his lips and pressed a gentle, lingering kiss to the sensitive skin between her fingers.

With the extent of his injuries, Laura had thought herself safe, but he was lighting fires too fast for her to extinguish. She gave him one of her best *you'd better behave* expressions.

He released her hand. And though the spark had been put out, its warmth lingered, slowly melting a small amount of the coldness around her heart.

The doctor pulled a penlight out of her smock pocket and leaned close to Troy's face. "Look straight ahead, please."

The doctor waved the light back and forth in front of his right eye. "How long have you two been together?" she asked, and Laura realized the woman was still under the impression she and Troy were an item.

Troy sighed. "It seems like forever in one sense, yet not very long in another. I guess time doesn't really matter when you've found the right one. Isn't that right, *angel face*?"

Embarrassed with his choice of endearments and further frustrated because he would not be serious, Laura felt the warmth in her cheeks turn a few degrees hotter. Was there no end to his foolishness? She caught him looking at her out the corner of his eyes.

"Continue looking forward please." The doctor moved the penlight to Troy's left eye. "I've often heard other couples say the same," she said, "about love and losing sight of time."

Then turning off the light, she stood and

dropped it back into her pocket. "You're going to have a bad headache for awhile. I'll give you some painkillers for the arm and rib, but take it easy and," she looked at Laura, "make sure he stays awake for at least twelve hours. Check on him about every two hours after that for the next twenty-four. If you notice any changes in his speech or mobility, get him back in here." She pulled out her prescription pad.

"What about, well, you know...?" Laura asked, thinking the best thing for her peace of mind would be for the doctor to give him something that would knock him out for the rest of her vacation.

The doctor paused in writing and glanced up. "I suggest, as far as sex goes, do what you two feel comfortable with."

With the prescription written and torn from the pad, she handed it to Troy. "For tonight perhaps, you might just consider snuggling up somewhere together and keeping warm, but again, if he falls asleep, wake him every two hours."

"But..." Laura held out her hand, but it was a useless gesture, for the doctor already turned away, dropping the curtain closed behind her.

"...we're not a couple," Laura finished weakly. She stared at the curtain then turned to Troy. His eyes were closed.

She was blindsided with the image of them snuggled lovingly in each other's embrace, on the couch, in front of the fire. An ache-filled longing tapped softly at the door of her heart.

'Little Miss Daydreamer...' she could hear Steve's faint whisper.

She looked away from Troy. If she ignored the tapping, perhaps Steve's voice would go away.

"Did you hear what the doctor said?" Troy's liquid smooth voice filled the silence in the small enclosure.

"About what?"

"About us having sex if we want."

"We're *not* having sex!" she whispered in frustration.

"But she said we could."

"No, she didn't. She said we could snuggle up together and keep warm."

"Okay." He sighed. "We'll just snuggle then."

"We're not snuggling either!"

"You're no fun."

"Does everything that's fun for you have sex involved?"

"Usually."

"You're impossible."

His every look, his every word was like a fireball thrown with amazing accuracy against her wall of ice. She had to get away from him, for that part of her that he'd awakened would like nothing more than to lie in his arms and feel his warm breath against her face as she surrendered to his kisses.

She stepped quickly toward the opening of the curtain and almost collided with the nurse who entered carrying several more papers. "I need to go over the aftercare instructions then he can dress and go home."

Laura tried to focus her attention on the step-by-step instructions as the nurse read them aloud, but she kept glancing toward Troy instead. Once again, his eyes were shut.

He's more frustrating than a child. Her gaze rolled like an ocean wave over his body. Taking in his pectoral muscles above the bandaging, the narrow hips and the long length of leg beneath the blanket, she had to concede, he was not a child, but very much a man, and a man intent on keeping her emotions in a constant state of unbalance.

Don't get emotionally involved with any man. A promise she had sworn to herself, after Steve. A promise she had kept for a year and a half. She wasn't about to change that now.

Emotional involvement led to physical involvement which led to more emotional involvement. Emotional involvement would mean opening her heart to unnecessary risk. And if there was one thing she knew about herself, she could never make love without giving her heart away totally and completely.

She'd come to believe it wasn't just any man who accepted the responsibility of caring for a woman's heart. No, she told herself, these men lived in the blanket of stardust that the Keeper of the Stars shook out every now and again to rescue a heart in danger of dying.

"Just sign here," the nurse said, breaking into Laura's thoughts. She handed Troy the papers.

He popped open one eye, took the pen and signed.

The nurse smiled at Laura as she separated

the papers and handed Troy his copies. "After you help your husband get dressed, we'll get him a wheelchair to take him out."

Laura opened her mouth to correct the nurse's assumption but clamped it shut again in resolution. What was the use?

The nurse walked out, closing the curtain behind her. Four words echoed in Laura's head. *Help him get dressed.* That meant touching him... getting close enough for his cologne to do some real damage... for the heat of his body to melt away more of her protective wall of ice. She swallowed hard and turned around.

"On your way out, could you send the nurse back in to help me get dressed?" His focus on her eyes was unwavering, his teasing tone gone.

"I-I can help you."

He shook his head carefully. "I'm not stupid, Laura. I know you can't stand the thought of touching me." His eyes narrowed. "I just want to know why?"

"I-I don't know what you mean," she stammered. She hadn't seen this serious side of him before, but intuition told her he was more of a threat to her like this than when he was with his flirting.

"What's wrong with me?" he asked, spreading his good arm wide with painful slowness for her inspection.

Nothing. Nothing's wrong with you. Yet she didn't say it.

He sniffed at his underarms then looked back at her. "Do I smell bad?"

I've never been near any man who smelled so wonderful.

"Is it my breath?"

I've never wanted to be kissed by a mouth that smelled so clean.

"Is my hair the wrong color?"

No.

"My eyes? Are my eyes the wrong color? Is it something else about me?" He sounded one question short of begging.

No, no- no! Laura closed her eyes, breaking contact with his. She shrugged helplessly.

"Can't you even answer one question?"

She heard his frustration fill and overflow into each question she'd left unanswered.

"Damn it, Laura, what are you afraid of?"

Laura flinched at his hostile tone, but it

became the one thing she grabbed on to, to pull herself out of the emotional quicksand of dejection. Looking him in the eye, she squared her shoulders. "I'm not afraid of anyone."

"I didn't say it was *someone*. A person, you can always run away from, but what's in here," he tapped his chest gently, "well, that's different. Those are the things that stay with you, that come back to haunt you."

His words slammed into her with such force that it nearly took her breath away. Eyes were the windows to the soul. Had she allowed him to look into her eyes too deeply? How many times had Steve's abuse come back to haunt her? Or the memory of Bobby's death?

With the protection of her heart becoming top priority, she hid her unsettling thoughts behind a mask of sarcasm. "So what's this? First you pretend to be my boyfriend and now you want to play my shrink?" Behind her eyes she felt the burn of unexpected tears, but she'd be damned if she let this Casanova cowboy make them spill over.

Troy sighed, his voice much calmer and restrained. "I was just saying—"

"It doesn't matter what you say. You don't

know me. You don't know anything about me, so save yourself a headache and don't try to psychoanalyze me. As a matter of fact, just leave me alone." She turned around and walked toward the curtain.

"Not until I find out what you're running from," he said.

Laura stopped and shot a glance over her shoulder. "Is that a threat?"

"When I make a threat, usually one person has more to lose than the other. When I make a promise, both parties benefit. You make the call."

Laura swallowed. She saw it as a definite threat. She looked at him a moment longer then stepped through the curtain.

"I'll see you back at the townhouse," he called out loudly, then grunted painfully.

CHAPTER SEVEN

LAURA RAPPED her knuckles lightly against Troy's bedroom door. What in the world had possessed her to take the graveyard shift?

Damn butterflies. She placed a hand over her stomach, hoping fear wouldn't chase her back to her room to lock the door and hide. But she knew there was nowhere to hide from her feelings.

She knocked again.

Still no answer.

She opened the door and peeked inside. "Troy, are you awake?"

A nightlight bathed the room in soft shadows. She glanced around. No Troy here. She closed the door, wondering where he'd gone.

The bathroom door hung open, but the light was off. Still, she reached out to knock. *Nothing.* Then she heard a noise downstairs.

Thick carpeting muffled the sound of her footsteps as they carried her down the stairs to the kitchen. She paused in the doorway. Troy stood at the counter with his back to her, wearing only a pair of maroon colored pajama bottoms. The butterflies in her stomach beat their wings in frantic frenzy.

By the faint glow from the stove light, she saw a bottle of *Seagram's Seven* sitting on the counter top beside him, but she became too caught up in the play of shadows on his back to pay much attention to anything else.

His pajama bottoms rode low on his hips, an outright dare to her imagination. Her eyes followed the valley of his spine up past the binding around his ribs. The flesh over his shoulder blade grew taut as he lifted a glass and threw down a shot of whiskey.

"What in the name of heaven do you think you're doing?" she whispered loudly, common sense sending the butterflies into hiding.

His hand paused in midair before he set the glass on the counter top. "Numbing the pain," he said without turning.

"Didn't the doctor give you medication for that?"

He turned. Even from a distance she could see discomfort in his eyes.

Amy Lynn

"Whiskey works better."

Laura strode to him and snatched up the bottle. "*Not* mixed with pain killers!" She opened the cabinet door and placed the bottle inside. She spun around to lecture him some more but he'd moved. He stood just in front of her with his cast wrist held against his stomach.

Something about him looked different.

Her gaze made a beeline from his sexy tussled hair, over his lips, chin and chest, all the way to the black trail of hair that disappeared behind the waistband of his low riding pajama bottoms, minus his boxer shorts. With her cheeks growing warm, she retraced the same path up, ending at his eyes.

"Where's your sling?"

"It was bugging the hell out of me."

He leaned forward until his chest came to within an inch of touching her face. She arched back against the counter, the edge digging into her back. He reached past her head to the cabinet door she'd just shut.

"You're not going to heal properly if you ignore the doctor's instructions," she told him.

"It's not the first time I've dislocated a shoulder or bruised a rib, and it won't be the last. I think I know how to take care of myself." He opened the cabinet door. "Trust me, whiskey works."

"I-I know something that works better," she croaked hoarsely, acutely aware if she breathed too deeply, their chests would touch.

He paused. Slowly he shut the cabinet door and braced his hand against it. Looking down into her eyes, he arched a black brow. "Only if it's the same thing I have in mind." His whispered breath teased her bangs and touched her cheek with a downy soft caress.

His face hung so close she could see individual whiskers on his chin and jaw line. The seductive scent of his cologne uncoiled from his warm flesh and wound its way around and beneath her nose, casting its spell over her senses and weakening her resolve. The implication of his words melted the tight knot of tension in her lower belly into warm desire.

"C-cards. We can play cards!" she said, hoping he didn't catch the quiver in her voice.

He broke eye contact. His gaze dropped to her mouth, then continued downward with more interest. "Strip poker?"

Laura glanced down. The top of her robe had fallen open, providing him with an unhindered view down the neckline of her satin nightshirt to the inner swell of her breast and the darkened valley between.

His slow smile bellowed flames, searing her heart. He leaned closer and raised his eyebrows as if hoping to catch a better view.

She gathered the front of her robe together protectively against her throat, her knuckles brushing against his chest in the process. The sexual awareness smoldering in the air between them sparked and ignited into something both hot and dangerous.

Laura found it difficult to swallow. "No..."

"No?" He dipped his head close to her neck and inhaled deeply. His breath, laced with the scent of whiskey, tickled the flesh just below her earlobe. "Is it at least something that involves the removal of clothing?"

"No," she said and quickly ducked under his outstretch arm before he could actually hear her pounding heartbeat. She turned to see him once more opening the cabinet door. Stepping forward she pushed it shut, forcing herself to stay focused, and hopefully in control of the situation.

"*No* more whiskey and *no* strip poker. Let's see what kind of board game I can dig out of the hall closet." She walked away on trembling legs, fighting the urge to fan her hand at her heated cheeks.

Laura cleared the coffee table and set up the Scrabble board. Troy sat on the couch. She sat on the floor across from him, the fireplace to her back. Between the firelight and a dim lamp they had enough light to see by but not enough to aggravate his headache.

Each picked up a wooden cube and turned it over. Troy won first play.

"What made you volunteer to baby sit for the late shift?" He laid down the pieces, spelling the word, PASSION.

Laura wrote down the points. "I slept away most of the afternoon. It only made sense." She spelled, FOOLISH.

"Then you're over your fear of being alone with me?" He lay down his squares, FORE.

Laura eyed his letters doubtfully. "Are you sure that's a word?"

"Positive." He gathered up several cubes to replace the ones he'd played.

Amy Lynn

She played her squares. POWER. "I told you I wasn't scared of anyone."

"So you said." He placed the word PLAY after the word FORE. It was a triple word play with a double letter score.

Laura placed her letters below the N in PASSION, spelling the word NEVER. She hid her smile. "So how long did you live in Montana?"

Troy returned with the word CARESS. "Seventeen years."

Laura was just as quick to lay down the word CASTLE. "Why so long?"

He looked up from rearranging his letters in his holder, and for the first time, Laura detected a pain that went beyond the physical, then it was gone. "The year my mother passed away, Rebel stayed with dad. I went to spend the summer with my aunt and uncle on their ranch. Just seemed like a nice play for a boy to grow up, so I stayed." He put his letters down. NAKED.

Something in his tone told her his reasons for staying held a deeper pain. She understood wanting to keep some things private. Taking a breath, she played the word ICE. "Any ex-wives or trail of broken hearts?"

"No ex's." Then he gave her a crooked

smile. "Though I'm sure there's plenty of the other." He played the word WEAK.

Laura frowned. *WEAK?* Was he referencing her?

Finally, all the wood pieces on the table had been gathered and Laura's turn came next. She looked at the letters lined up on her letter holder. She would have to connect it to S in the word CARESS already on the board. It would give her a triple word score with two double letter points. She glanced at the score pad. She knew making this word would win the game even if he did get the last turn.

But this word made her hesitate. *SURRENDER*

Winning would mean losing, because it wasn't just a word anymore. Too much had been laid out on the table between them, and this one word would not let her walk away feeling like a winner.

She glanced at him, took in his handsome face, and those breathtaking gray eyes, his perfectly proportioned physique. No, if she played the word, she would risk losing everything.

Her shoulders lifted then dropped. "I don't

have anything else, sorry."

His look turned suspicious. "You have seven squares left. You can't spell anything else?"

Laura caught her bottom lip between her teeth and shook her head, "No."

"Let me see." He reached for her wooden holder.

"Wait!" Seized by panic, she pushed his hand back. "There is one small word."

The word wouldn't be enough to give her the game points, but she could end the game knowing she hadn't really lost. She picked up two squares and placed them on the board. RUN. She grinned and looked up. "There."

Laughing, he shook his head then laid down his letters for the last play of the game. STAY.

"Care to play again?" he asked, gathering up the wooden pieces.

Laura picked up her letter holder and dumped the remaining game pieces into the box with the others. "And have you come out on top again? Not a chance."

"I'd be more than happy to finish with you on top."

The letter holder fell from Laura's hand and

clattered onto the tabletop. His comment stoked the heat in her cheeks to an unbearable degree. She understood his meaning.

Suddenly, all the things she had been aware of but fought to keep in check came crashing forward in her mind.

They were alone. The others were sound asleep upstairs. It was snowing outside. There was a romantic fire burning. It was just the two of them, and he was half-naked already. A man and a woman and a whole lot of sexual tension in the air.

"You're not behaving," she said, diverting her gaze.

"Does that scare you?"

"How many times do I have to say it? I'm not afraid of you."

"Then tell me you're not afraid of yourself."

"That's absurd. Why would I be afraid of myself?" She stood, moving closer to the fireplace and farther from him.

Troy eased back against the sofa. He stretched his good arm along the back, letting his legs fall open in a relaxed manner.

Laura fought to control her wandering

gaze. Though she knew it was just the cut of his pajama bottoms, the tented crease down the front teased her highly charged imagination. Something she didn't need at the moment.

He shrugged his good shoulder. "Maybe you're scared of your own needs."

"Needs?" She hugged her arms about her middle. "The only need I have is for you to show a little self-control."

"I'm a man with very healthy needs. Because of that, you think I lack self-control?"

"That's exactly what I think."

The next moment passed in uncomfortable silence. Nervously, Laura shifted her weight to her other foot.

"When was the last time you kissed a man? Hell, Laura, when was the last time you let a man kiss you?"

You, I almost let you. Laura raised her chin. "I don't make satisfying my sexual needs top priority in life. I can control myself."

Troy's laughter rang out. "Oh yes, that's right. We have the Great Ice Princess here. Whenever the situation starts to heat up, you run away, emotionally and physically, to hide behind the safety of your cold castle wall. Well remember, darling, when you're standing outside the flame, life is not living, it's just surviving." He misquoted a line from an old country song. "So tell me, Laura, are you living life or just surviving? Is there a heart of unbridled passion beating behind those cold walls?"

Laura frowned. His statement hit too close to home. He'd pieced together her words in their Scrabble game perfectly.

"I'm done listening to your nonsense. I'm going back to bed. I'm sure you can find something to do by yourself to stay awake." She rushed past the couch.

He reached out and caught her wrist, halting her escape. "You're the one out of control, and you don't even know it."

Laura stared at his hand then looked him in the eye. "How do you figure?"

"Let me kiss you. I'll prove it."

Butterflies stirred and beat their wings wildly. "Go to hell."

"Running away just proves I'm right."

That stopped her. She'd like nothing better than to shake the branches of his arrogance tree and send his ego crashing to the ground. "It proves nothing."

"Care to make a little wager?" He released her arm.

She should have walked away, but she didn't. "Wager? What kind of wager?"

"I'll bet my control against yours."

"You're crazy."

"Wha'daya say Laura, just a little kiss."

Though she had no intention of doing it, curiosity shoved control out the door. "What do I win?"

He flashed a smile. "*If* you win, I'll back off."

She cast him a doubtful glance.

"I promise. Wha'daya say?"

"And you, what is it you hope to win?" she asked, unsure if she really wanted to know.

"If I win, be my housekeeper once a week until I'm completely healed."

That's it? A housekeeper? Not the answer she expected from him. The guy had definite charm, but she felt disappointed with his lack of imagination.

Suddenly an image flashed in her mind. "*If* I lose, which I won't, you aren't expecting me to wear one of those French maid uniforms, are you?"

"Wear whatever you like. Or nothing at all. Your choice." The corners of his eyes crinkled with humor.

It was just a kiss, *one kiss*. Perhaps if she faced her fear of it, got it over with, she could put it behind her and get some peace of mind. And if he got his kiss, he'd leave her alone.

"Only a kiss, nothing else."

"Nothing," he echoed. "In fact we'll add the condition that we can't touch in any other way. Would that make you feel better?"

"Just a kiss?" She wanted to be certain. Everything needed to be laid out in black and white. The only gray, she wanted to see was the color of his eyes.

"But it's got to be a ten second kiss, like a lover," Troy added.

"Five seconds," Laura returned.

"Fifteen."

She found no mercy in his eyes. "Ten it is."

This last year of practicing self-control would now be put to the test. She could do this.

Troy patted the tabletop.

Laura raised an eyebrow.

He laughed softly, setting off a chain reaction of shivers down her spine. "It'll be easier for you, and less painful for me," he explained.

Laura moved carefully between him and the coffee table and sat down. She checked her robe again to the tune of his quiet laugher. His confidence irked her. About to close her robe up tight and cover her exposed thighs, she threw caution to the wind. *What the hell.*

Unwavering, she looked him in the eye. "My control against yours, only a kiss, and no other touching, right?"

"That's it." His dimpled smile looked more cocky than sincere.

Without looking away, she reached up and loosened the neckline of her robe letting it gap open to expose the deep V of her nightshirt. He blinked but didn't break eye contact.

Reaching down she separated and threw open the bottom of her robe over her thighs. The hem of her nightshirt teased more than covered the smooth, tanned flesh of her inner thighs. Still, his gaze remained unwavering. The only sign he showed that her actions had affected him was in the hard bob of his Adam's apple.

She purposely moistened her lips with the

tip of her tongue.

His gaze dropped to her mouth.

Oh yeah, piece of cake. She smiled. "Just a kiss, right?"

"Just a kiss," he answered. "I won't lay a hand on you. Now quit stalling. In ten seconds it'll all be over."

Laura opened her mouth to remark on his comment when the faint scent of his cologne touched her. An invisible band wrapped around her chest. Breathing became difficult. The sensation of lightheadedness came over her. The control she was sure of only a moment ago vanished, and now it was too late to back out without being unmercifully teased.

"Ready?" he asked again.

Knowing better than to trust her voice, Laura nodded while thinking the dimple in his cheek appeared *too* quickly.

She leaned forward and closed her eyes. Her lips pressed with trepidation against his. Their warmth surprised her. The first contact rumbled the foundation supporting the wall around her heart.

One, two, ten! She sat back. "Well?"

"What the hell was that supposed to be?" He choked.

"It was a kiss." She rose quickly from her seat, but his hand around her wrist stopped her escape. She gave his hand a pointed glance, then him. "A-ah, there was to be no other contact, remember? You touched me. You lose."

The gentle pull of his hand set her back down. "No, that's not the kiss we agreed upon. Shame on you, Laura. My grandmother kissed me like that. If you remember, we agreed, a lover's kiss. For ten seconds."

She should have run when she had the chance. How could she have failed to see, though the matches he'd tossed at her had small flames, several of them thrown at once created an inferno?

Feel annoyed, she told herself. She swallowed hard, closed her eyes, and leaned forward again. Annoyance, not passion or desire. Ten seconds of feeling annoyed. She could do it.

Her lips fell upon his like a downy feather carried through the air on a warm breeze. *One Mississippi, two Mississippi.* Her heart pounded like a kettledrum. *Three Mississippi, four...*

This time the scent of his cologne wound around her head, conjuring up a spell meant to interfere with her thought process. *Three Mississippi.*

From some deep, recess of her heart came a stirring. Churning slowly at first, then gathering force, like the winds of a storm. *Two Mississippi.* Her mouth opened against his, instinctively seeking a response.

He opened his mouth.

Her tongue slipped in. Her mouth slanted across his. *Three Mississippi, no wait, four Mississippi.*

A moan rumbled from deep within his throat and churned the winds of emotions, shaking loose a boldness she'd so desperately tried to hold in check.

Her tongue found his, but had to coax a response. Something within her shattered. Like breaking ice. She wasn't sure. All she knew was that she couldn't stop.

Like a platter of delicacies set before her, she nibbled and fed, pulling gently on his lips with her teeth, kissing the corners of his mouth, then moving to feast from within again.

Four Mississippi. Her hands and fingers wound themselves wantonly through his soft, thick hair, trying to draw his head closer, driven by a need to fill the emptiness that cried out from within her.

Four Mississippi. Then, as if passing through the eye of the storm to the other side of the whirlwind, the realization came to her. Troy's cast arm remained against his abdomen, his other upon his thigh.

The dizziness in her head slowly settled, pulling her back from her fairytale moment.

Four Mississippi. Still the kiss seemed as if it would never end. When it finally did, she rested her forehead against his shoulder, catching her breath and waiting for the spinning winds to set her safely down before she faced the 'I told you so' look in his eyes.

She felt his cheek brush against the side of her head. His voice, gentle and concerned, touched her ear. "Are you going to be all right?"

Her answer was carried on a shaky sigh. "Yeah, I'll be all right." But she knew nothing would be all right, ever again.

For several moments, he allowed her to remain with him, taking time to collect herself. When she sat back, she braved a glance into his eyes, but all she found in the dusky gray depths was a strange look of wonderment.

"Well, Mr. Hawke." Laura stood on shaky legs and adjusted her robe. "You got your lover's kiss and you've won yourself a housekeeper. Now, if you don't mind, I'll leave you to your own devices. I'm going back to my room." She walked away, holding herself with as much dignity she could muster.

His response to her kiss had been passive. But the blow to her pride came in the realization that the sounds she'd heard coming from deep within his throat had been controlled grunts of pain, not of passion.

He'd tried to quell the pain *her* loss of control had caused to his ribs and shoulders, and she knew he could not have shown more control than that.

CHAPTER EIGHT

SHE WAS RUNNING from him, again.

She'd been looking out over the moss-covered castle wall when he approached. He sat astride a magnificent white stallion, its coat as shiny as its rider's armor. A true knight, a true gentleman, he held his helmet in the crook of his arm, and she could see that he was not the one who usually came. She watched in longing as a breeze fingered its way through his thick black hair.

But those eyes, those smoky gray eyes could see into her very soul, and they locked onto hers from below and would not let her go. They told her he was coming for her, and he would climb the castle wall if she did not let him in through the gate.

He called her name. His voice gently caressed her senses. With a sob, she shook her head. She wanted to speak, but couldn't. She tried to shout that she couldn't let him in; she was too terrified. The castle walls kept her safe. He should go away and leave her alone. He would not be happy with what he found when he rescued her.

Keeper of the Stars

He called her name again and began to scale the wall. She turned and ran. Her hair fell loose from its binding and flowed wild and free behind her. Sensing she didn't have much time left, she tried to hide her soul. For that's what the one that came before had tried to destroy.

From behind her came a sound. In overwhelming panic, she looked back. He climbed over the wall. Again he called out to her. And still, she ran. He followed with steps that were sure and unhurried.

Like a frightened doe she glanced about, this way and that. There was nowhere to run, nowhere to hide. In the next instant, she found herself in a long windowless corridor. She whirled around to find him standing before her.

He raised his hand to her. She brought her own up to block an expected blow, but none came. He only whispered her name, softly and lovingly.

Uncertainty and confusion replaced her fear. Slowly, she lowered her arm. He held out his hand to her. All he seemed to be asking was for her to put her hand in his.

The longing to do so became so great it turned into a physical ache. Still, putting her hand in his would mean walking out from behind the castle wall, a lonely place, but she felt safe here.

His breath touched her as he whispered her name. She closed her eyes and yielded her face to the warmth of his soul. This new warmth felt good.

He reached out and cupped his palm against her cheek. She whimpered and turned her lips into his palm, kissing in surrender to that protective hand, his voice gentle and reassuring against her ear.

"Ah, my sweet Laura, I will never hurt you. I will forever guard your heart as a knight should, and I shall be here waiting. Always. Forever waiting.

Laura woke with a start to the soft click of a door closing. With her heart still pounding from the effects of the dream, she sat up and peered through the darkness, half expecting to see the handsome knight. Though certain she was alone, his presence and scent seemed to linger faintly in the air.

She reached for the comforter but found it kicked in a heap at the foot of the bed. Drawing her knees to her chest, she wrapped her arms around herself and slowly rocked back and forth. The motion soothed her, and though this hadn't been one of her usual nightmares, it left her feeling just as disturbed.

This time, it wasn't Steve who scaled the

wall or reached out his hand to strike her. Troy had been the one who'd called her name.

Laura laid her cheek against her knees. "Which will betray me in the end?" she whispered into the darkness. "My body or my heart?"

From the room next to hers came a scraping sound followed by footsteps. She glanced at the clock and dropped her forehead onto her knees. Only an hour had elapsed since she'd left Troy alone downstairs.

She was surprised she'd fallen asleep at all, certain the memory of the kiss and her drained emotions would keep her restless until dawn.

A loud thump sounded from his room again. Laura shut her eyes and rocked harder. She didn't want to go to his room to investigate. She wanted to stay within the safety of her own four walls. Hiding kept her safe.

Thump!

She covered her ears. If she didn't listen, perhaps Rebecca would wake up and attend to him. Maybe he just stubbed his toe. It would serve him right for tricking her with the bet.

Scrape! Thump!

Laura mouthed a curse and swung her legs

over the edge of the bed, torn between letting him be or going to see what he was doing. A couple more good thumps and he'd have everyone in the house awake.

Laura held her breath for a moment and prayed.

Silence.

She waited another moment. More silence.

Thump!

Springing to her feet she hurried to her door, but stopped short. She turned and walked back to the bed. She didn't want to go. Yet her conscience wouldn't let her ignore the possibility that he might have caused himself more injury. Her imagination ran wild with him lying on the floor, unable to get up. Perhaps he fell and struck his head, knocking himself out. Or what if she went to his room and felt the aching need for his kiss again, or worse yet, the burning desire for something more?

She didn't want to go. But she knew she couldn't stay.

Moving to her door, and with a thin measure of bravado, she left the safety of her room and knocked once before opening his door. "Troy, are you okay?"

Through the faint glow of the nightlight she could see him seated across the room against the windowsill with his chin to his chest. So as not to wake the others, she slipped inside and shut the door. "Troy?"

Her whisper brought his head up. She saw he held his cast wrist against his ribs. Concern pushed aside caution, and she went to him, forgetting the need to stay outside his aura of sexual energy.

"What did you do?" she asked.

He nodded toward the bed. "I dropped my watch."

Laura turned to look, her eyes widening in disbelief. "You tried to move the bed?"

Not waiting for his answer, she went over and lifted the bed skirt off the floor. She could see a faint glimmer of metal some distance back. She'd have to get on her hands and knees and stretch to reach it.

She brought her hands down to pull aside the bottom of her robe so it wouldn't get in the way, but instead of her robe, she touched bare thigh. Her heart leapt. In her concern for him, she'd left her room without her robe. The white satin nightshirt was modest enough, but if she were to bend down, her rear-end would be left sticking up in the air toward him.

She dropped the bed skirt and walked back to face him. "We'll get your watch in the morning. If there's nothing else you need, then I'm going back to my room."

"Stay."

Run.

His quiet request and her unspoken response made her wonder if the Scrabble game had somehow been a premonition of things to come.

Like a cowboy well practiced in the art of corralling an untrusting mustang, he placed his legs on either side of her.

The action didn't go unnoticed. With her next heartbeat, the faint scent of his cologne touched her, and she realized she'd stepped within his aura.

An element of danger skipped up her spine, like a stone on water, and she felt its rippling effect spreading out, touching every nerve in her body. In two more heartbeats, he reached out and caught the material of her nightshirt between his thumb and forefinger. The contact caused her stomach muscles to contract.

Common sense told her to get out, fast. Her other senses warned not to linger a moment longer or she would not be leaving until morning.

"Why did you come?" he asked quietly.

"I–you were making too much noise."

"Not what I meant. What did you really come searching for, Laura?" he asked again.

She didn't know what to say. How could she put into words that which had no verbal response? Looking into his gray eyes, she realized any answer she gave wouldn't matter, for mirrored on that gray surface, one need reflected back: her need to be rescued. Its intensity astonished her. And suddenly, the smoldering ashes of desire ignited into a burning flame.

Too long exhausted from trying to keep it under control, and too weary to fight against it anymore, she felt a spark jump the wall. In that instant, fire and ice stood face to face.

The look in his eyes turned to one of wonder.

He knew.

She watched his gaze drop with purpose, lingering for several moments on her mouth. A pleasurable tingle filled her breast and tightened her nipples into hardened buds.

As if he too were aware of the changes taking place, his gaze dipped lower. She took a slow, deep breath. Her breast lifted against her nightshirt, intensifying her need to be touched.

"Troy..." the soft plea hung in the air between them.

Their gazes met.

She knew then, she wouldn't see the other side of his bedroom door until morning. The knowledge left her weakened, drained of all her resolve. She allowed him to pull her forward until she stood between his open thighs.

"Are you sure you'll find what you're searching for in here?" he asked quietly.

Laura knew he was giving her a chance to turn around and leave.

"Will there be any harm in looking?" she whispered back.

Silence stretched for eternity. Finally, he answered, "No harm, just a hope that you find what you've lost."

What had she lost? What was she hoping to find? Would she find him to be her knight in shining armor, her protector, a wish made on a falling star? Would she find the courage to trust again?

He leaned his head alongside her neck and breathed in deeply. "You smell like a wish come true."

His warm breath caressed her, and Laura closed her eyes, unable to hold back a sigh. "And you smell like you've been into the whiskey again."

"Maybe a little." He moved his head to the other side of her neck where he placed a feather-light kiss.

She trembled. "I told you...no more...whiskey."

He pulled back and gazed into her eyes. She watched a sparkle of humor ripple across the surface of his eyes.

"You should have kept a better eye on me instead of running away," he said.

"You shouldn't have kissed me," she murmured.

"Ah, but it was *you* who kissed me."

"Only because you tricked me."

Troy brushed his cheek against hers then placed another light kiss beneath her ear. "I was just seeing to your needs."

"I told you, I...can control...those needs." She moaned softly as he pressed his lips to her neck.

"I know you can," he breathed, working his kisses around to the front of her neck. Her head fell back, allowing him full access to her throat. She moaned again, this time long and low, filled with sensuous delight.

His hand moved around to settle onto the low dip of her back. With a gentle kneading motion, he slowly guided her forward until she found herself pressed against his erection straining against his pajama bottoms. She could feel his heat burn through the satin material of her nightshirt.

"Are you trying to seduce me?" she whispered weakly.

"Not if you don't want me to." His voice was strained but controlled.

He placed a kiss into the hollow at the base of her throat and pressed her more purposefully against him. Her groan echoed both pleasure and frustration.

Laura raised a hand and ran her fingers through the velvety thickness of his hair, tempted to grab onto a handful, if only to keep her balance. "What would you say...if I told you I didn't...want you to?"

Troy planted a gentle, unhurried kiss just below the hollow of her throat, soliciting another soft, low sigh of pleasure from her. "I'd tell you that..." He placed another kiss lower still.

She whimpered.

"...all you'd have to do..." His lips brushed the rising swell of her breast. "...is to tell me..."

She groaned in anticipation.

"...to stop," he finished as his open mouth covered her. His tongue traced around and over the satin material covering her nipple. She arched back and caught her breath at the sensation.

Her body wrestled with her mind for the right to fulfill a long suppressed need. She had her answer to the question she'd asked herself in the darkness of her room. Her body would be the one to betray her.

In that instant, all the hungers she had kept locked away for so long broke loose from their chains of restraint. She couldn't stop her knees from buckling. His hand at her back held her up and pushed her with more urgency against him.

Laura felt the world tip and, in this moment, in this room, in his arms, she was held between the past and the future. She parted her lips. He pulled her forward and covered her mouth with his, taking the sound of her frustration into his own throat.

His open mouth slanted across hers and she welcomed him in. Their tongues touched, parted then touched again. Her throaty moans played out a melody, turning the kiss into a dance.

In that secret darkness where lovers first met, their tongues caressed and stroked, slowly moving around the other, teasing, tempting, seducing.

But more than her tongue had a need to be joined with him in this dance for lovers. In answer to the gentle thrust of her hips, Troy repositioned his seating against the windowsill to better accommodate her search.

He lifted the back hem of her nightshirt and brushed his hand over her satin panties before moving on to caress her hip and thigh. A long deep moan rumbled up from his throat before he tore his mouth away.

"Nooo..." she whimpered, almost collapsing.

In the next instant, his mouth was at her breast again. She sighed, momentarily pacified.

Troy groaned. She could sense his growing frustration with their barrier of clothing. She pulled his head up to kiss his mouth again, but knew neither of them would find what they were looking for leaning against a bedroom windowsill.

He ended the kiss, and breathing hard, leaned his forehead against hers. "Wrap your arms around my neck."

Laura brought her hands up to comply, but stopped. "You're hurt. You can't carry me."

Troy pulled back and looked at her. "I'm just going to help you walk."

Laura touched his cheek with a trembling hand and gave him a tender smile. "You don't have to do that."

The dimple in his cheek surfaced. "I do if your legs are trembling as bad as your hands." He turned his head and placed a gentle kiss inside her palm. Her heart fluttered wildly, for it was just as she had done to him in her dream.

His mouth covered hers again. He brought his hand up and gently cradled the back of her head. Standing, he slowly guided her backward toward the bed.

It only took a moment for her to realize just how right he'd been. Though the magic of his mouth had already sufficiently weakened her whole body, by the time the back of her legs touched the bed, she felt ready to collapse.

Still kissing her, Troy placed a knee upon the bed and laid her back on crumpled sheets. Laura heard his quiet grunt of pain. She ended the kiss and gently touched his arm. "Your shoulder—"

"I'll be okay," he told her with a ragged breath. "Unless," his brows drew into a frown. "Unless you're having second thoughts. If you are, Laura, you need to tell me now." He leaned down and kissed her forehead tenderly. "I don't want you to have any regrets."

Steve's abuse fought to surface in the form of murky memories, but she placed a finger against Troy's lips. "I'm not having second thoughts." She glanced away. "I suppose I'm just nervous. It's been a long time for me. I don't want to..." her voice softened, "...disappoint you."

She could feel the intensity of his gaze as he silently studied her. Was *he* having second thoughts?

Keeper of the Stars

His soft laughter was unexpected. "I'm afraid that in my present condition I'll be the one to disappoint you. I can't promise you much in the way of performance, but I can promise you one of two things. We'll either reach the stars of heaven together, or you'll wind up laughing your head off at me trying to get us there."

Laura smiled. Like a magic wand in a fairytale, his humor passed over her and her nervousness disappeared. "The stars of heaven. It sounds like a nice place to visit."

Troy nuzzled her neck. "Heaven shouldn't be too far away. I already have an angel in my arms."

"You say the sweetest things." Laura sighed with a smile and closed her eyes.

His kiss was long and thorough. Still her body wanted more. She wanted to be touched, caressed, and filled to overflowing.

He lay on his side, supporting his weight with his good arm. Laura turned on her side to face him. Looking into his eyes she felt secure, protected. She ran her fingertip lightly across his eyelids, then down his cheek. Her thumb stroked his lips. He smiled, catching it playfully between his teeth. He ran the tip of his tongue around it before releasing it.

He kissed the curve of her breast filling the open V of her neckline before moving on to tease her satin covered nipples.

'You'll never be able to give him what he wants, Laura,' Steve's condescending tone crept its way into her thoughts. *'You're tainted and used, good for no one but me.'*

The memories stilled her. A lone tear escaped and rolled down her cheek.

Troy's head came up. "Laura, what's wrong?"

Laura turned her head, trying to hide her anguish.

Troy rose over her, his voice filled with concern. "Please, Laura, tell me why you're crying." His soft plea tore through her heart. "If you've changed your mind, just tell me. I won't be angry. As much as I want you, it's not worth seeing you cry. Come to me willingly or not at all."

Behind closed eyes, Laura saw how Steve had turned her dreams into nightmares. He always hurt her.

But tonight, for the first time, there was

Keeper of the Stars

another. She opened her eyes. Troy watched her, patiently waiting. He was her knight in shining armor. He hid nothing, and he hadn't come to hurt, but to heal.

She didn't want to remember Steve anymore, not here. Not in the soft shadows of this room. Perhaps if she let Troy take her from the castle, Steve would never find her again. She could start tonight, with this moment, making new dreams. Trusting again.

Yes! That's what she would do. Go with Troy. Ride fast and far away. He would protect her. He'd told her so.

With a new purpose, Laura boldly reached out and pulled his mouth down to hers again. Toward the warm and twinkling stars of heaven they rode. Higher and higher, until they topped the crest together. Laura held on tight, crying out at the beauty and warmth of the world on the other side.

Only later, after they had taken a more leisurely ride, did she fall asleep in the protective warmth of her knight's arms.

CHAPTER NINE

TROY STARED out the bedroom window into the quickly fading, star filled sky. He should have fallen asleep not long after Laura, but troubled thoughts made him restless. He stretched his neck from side to side trying to work out a kink then steeled himself against the pain of a deep breath.

Turning away from the widow he walked to the nightstand where he picked up the bottle of painkillers. His eyes scanned the label. *Take one every four hours as needed for pain.*

Popping the lid off with the thumb of his right hand, he tipped his head back and gently shook the bottle until three capsules rolled into his mouth. He then washed them down with the half-empty glass of lukewarm water.

He was hesitant to climb back into bed. Afraid of waking Laura and shatter his own dream, he savored the next few minutes just looking down at her.

Keeper of the Stars

Though her lips were still slightly swollen from his kisses, her features seemed softer and more relaxed, showing nothing of the stress and uncertainty that he'd seen earlier.

Sometime during their lovemaking, much to his delight, she had untied her braid. And now, like a pot of honey that had tipped over, her hair flowed across their pillows and over her body. His gaze rode the pale waves pausing on her breast peeking out from between the thick strands. The unexpected view brought a stirring in his loins.

She had given him more than he dared, or hoped, and with an eagerness that stole his breath away. No matter how much self-control he prided himself in, it was the simple act of her crying out his name at her climax that had toppled him over the edge and caused him to melt within her.

He'd been given one week to break through her wall of defense, her need to run. Instead, in two days she'd found her way into his heart. He'd fallen in love with her.

Returning to the window, he brushed the curtain aside. Was there really magic in a falling star? He'd long ago stopped believing so, for no matter how many times he'd wished on one, his wishes never came true. So why had this one been granted, and why now?

Destiny? Fate? He always believed a man determined his own destiny. Yet from the moment he'd inhaled this woman's sweet fragrance and looked into her eyes, he knew where his destiny lay.

But what about her? What he felt was too real for him to be lost in this alone. Still, something he couldn't quite put a finger on nagged at him. She had come willing enough, but for what reason?

She hadn't told him she loved him. And though she'd called out his name repeatedly, she never said the words, for he had listened for them. Not even the powerful force of passion had caused them to slip from her lips.

Just one night to love her. Wasn't that what he'd wished for? Still...

He scanned the expanse of the heavens, hoping for another star. This time the wish would not be for just one night, but a lifetime of nights to spend with her.

Troy rubbed the stubble on his jaw. His next breath pulled into his nostrils the sweet aroma her passion had left on his hand. His body responded naturally to her scent, and he knew that he never wanted her to share with another man what she had shared with him tonight.

He looked up once more. There would be no star to wish on tonight. He would have to win her heart on his own.

Troy left the window and walked back to the bed where he gazed down at her sleeping form once more. As if sensing his presence, Laura stirred and sighed. Her hand reached out and brushed across the vacant spot beside her. Slowly her eyes fluttered open. She gave him a sleepy smile.

"Are you leaving me?" she sighed, closing her eyes again.

Troy climbed in beside her. He couldn't keep his breath from catching as he leaned over her and placed a gentle kiss upon her lips. "I'll never leave you, Laura. I'll always be near, waiting."

She raised her arm around his neck and opened her mouth against his. Like a drop of morning dew rolling toward the end of a leaf, her sigh came long and slow. Her body moved with one purpose against him.

Before he let himself get lost in her again, he buried his face in the soft thick tresses of her hair, closed his eyes and wished away the first faint glow of morning.

***

'Laura, Laura!'

At the repeated calling of her name, Laura began her slow rise from contented sleep, vaguely aware something was different.

'Laura, Laura, wished on the stars, but what's it going to get her? More ugly scars.'

Laura stirred restlessly with Steve's whispered words intruding into the mists of her tender dreams.

'What a hell of a mess you've gotten yourself into this time, little tramp. Did you think having him would make me go away? You played the part so well, but now the morning light will show him what you really are. A whore, Laura. But you're my whore, and you always will be. Whore, whore...'

Laura jerked awake. Though her breathing was labored, she lay still, and focused on her surroundings. She was lying on her side nestled against Troy. Like a cocoon wrapped around a branch in its last moments of metamorphosis, her arm rested across his chest and her right leg propped over his groin, making her aware that neither of them had on any clothes.

The sheet just covered her thigh. Her naked breast pressed against the white bandages around his chest.

At once, the dreams of last night came flooding into her mind. She lifted her head to stare into the face of reality just inches away.

Reality was Troy. No knight in shining armor. Just a man with healthy needs. Isn't that what he'd said? How could she have been so foolish to believe anything more?

Luke's voice called from the hallway. "Laura, are you awake? I fixed you breakfast in bed."

Laura heard her bedroom door open. "Hey," Luke called out. "She's not in here."

"See if Troy has seen her this morning." Rebecca's voice carried up from downstairs.

Now Luke's going to see you, Laura. Finally, he's going to know you for the little tramp you really are.

Laura panicked and made a desperate attempt to pull away from her sleeping companion with the hope of getting to the door before Luke came in. But Troy's hold around her shoulder tightened, halting her escape.

Luke's footsteps stopped just outside the bedroom door a moment before he tapped lightly. "Hey, Troy, have you seen Laura?"

'Run, Laura, run before Luke sees you naked. Your dead brother entrusted his son to your care. If he could see you now, what would he say? He'd call you a whore, Laura. A whore...'

This time Laura managed to extract herself from Troy's hold and was just beginning to sit up on the side of the bed when she heard the soft click of the door opening.

"Troy, are you awake?" Luke called again.

'Too late!'

With a small cry of alarm, Laura scrambled to cover herself with part of the sheet without pulling it completely off Troy.

Luke strolled into the room, carrying the breakfast-laden tray but froze in mid-stride at her surprised cry. If the moment weren't so traumatic, she would have found the expression on his face worthy of a good laugh.

Laura turned and hit the heel of her palm against Troy's good shoulder. "Wake up, Troy!"

she ground out between clenched teeth.

Troy opened his eyes and looked at her. Clearing his throat, he glanced past her to Luke and threw the boy a slight nod of acknowledge. "Morning, Luke." His tone was casual, as if waking every morning beside her was a normal occurrence for him.

She shot a glance to Luke and watched a smile stretch across the boy's face.

"Guess I'll go get Troy some breakfast, too." Luke set the tray on the desk just inside the door.

"Luke." Laura stopped him. "No more breakfast. Leave now, and close the door behind you."

With a good-humored salute, Luke turned around, the ear-to-ear grin still plastered across his face. When he reached the doorway, he turned one last time, looked at Troy and gave him the thumbs up then pulled the door shut behind him.

"Hey, you guys!" Luke yelled, retreating down the hall. You're never gonna believe where I found Laura!"

'Now everyone's going to know about you.'

Laura scrambled from the bed, desperate to

escape Steve's haunting voice echoing in her head. With one quick swoop she pulled the sheet from Troy and wrapped it around herself in an attempt to hide her nakedness.

'Whore, whore, always playing whore'.

"I have to go," she said, her voice full of panic.

Troy moved from his side of the bed, his voice stern. "Laura, don't do this. Don't run away."

Laura froze for a moment. He thought she was running away from *him*. He didn't understand. He wouldn't. And she couldn't explain. She knew she had to stand up to Steve's memory sometime. Deal with her past. But now wasn't the time. Not here, not in the room where she and Troy had shared so much last night. She couldn't let her memories of Steve ruin that, too.

Laura kicked at the pooling length of sheet in front of her feet and began searching the floor. "Where's my shirt. I-I have to go," she stammered, fighting back the betraying burn of tears, refusing to look at him.

"Why?"

"Because I never should have come here last night." Because of Steve, were the words she wished she could say.

'You've got that right, honey. You're my whore, not his.'

She heard the soft brush of Troy's footsteps against the carpet. She turned. He was reaching out for her. Like a bridle shy mustang, she bolted away, almost tripping over the sheet entangling around her feet.

"Don't touch me!"

'That's not what you were telling him last night, was it, little tramp? With each second she stayed, Steve's voice grew stronger.

"Don't... please, Troy, don't touch me," Laura stated more firmly. If he touched her she'd collapse, she just knew it.

Troy stopped abruptly. His hand dropped to his side.

She focused on his face, but the black stubble on his jaw reminded her of the chafing along the inside of her thighs. And the lock of hair that fell down over his forehead, reminded her of how she'd hung on to him when the scratching stubble moved higher, driving her wild.

Even now her mind joined league with her body to betray her again. Memories of his touch and kisses passed uncensored through her mind.

'You're sick and pathetic with a dirty mind, Laura!' Steve taunted.

She had to get out. "I-I need to go."

She half turned but then stopped as she caught a glimpse of her reflection in the dresser mirror. Good lord, she barely recognized herself.

'That's right, Laura take a good look. That's what a dirty little whore looks like.'

Holding the sheet protectively against her breast her unbound hair flowed in wild abandonment in a thick mass of soft tangled waves over her shoulders and down her back. Her cheeks were awash with a light blush. She could have been playing the role in a movie as the seductive innocent.

But she wasn't a seductress. Nor an innocent. She was a woman haunted by nightmares of abuse and guilt, and as long as Steve kept her held tightly in the clutches of that fear, she could never trust being with another.

"Where will you go, Laura? How long will you run?" Troy quietly challenged.

A tremor passed through her as Troy spoke, for his was the voice that filled her ear with tender whispers during the night. But now, she was afraid to listen to anything he had to say, for that's how this mess had started. She'd let herself become intoxicated on the bourbon smooth sound of his voice.

"Whatever I decide to do, I'll do it alone, just like I've been doing all along," she said with a catch in her voice.

She turned in a circle, still glancing about the floor. Her search turned frantic as she realized she was losing the battle of holding back her tears.

"What are you looking for, Laura?"

She spun away. His nakedness almost became her undoing, for even now, she could still feel him inside her, taking her again and again to the stars of heaven. She fought back a moan of longing.

'You can't have him, Laura,' Steve's voice echoed. *'You're mine.'*

"I-my," her voice broke and a tear rolled down her cheek. Feeling helpless, she shook her head. "My shirt. Where's my nightshirt?"

Through blurred vision, Laura watched him stop short of reaching her. "Please, Troy. Don't touch me," she repeated.

"I only want to help."

'A naked knight? Where's his shining armor now, you stupid little...'

"Then, damnit, Troy, help me by putting some clothes on!"

"What's this now?" Troy snapped. "Suddenly you can't stand the sight of me? You had no problem with that or touching me just hours ago."

Laura flinched at his words, for now there was no wall to deflect the piercing pain that shot through her heart. If she let him touch her again, she would be lost forever, and Steve would never let her rest. That thought frightened her most of all. "Where's my shirt?"

"To hell with your shirt! You're not leaving until we get this settled." With his good hand, Troy worked himself into his pajama bottoms.

'He's getting angry, Laura. He's going to hit you!' Steve's words rang out within her head.

Laura moved around to the end of the bed. "There's nothing to settle." With one hand holding the sheet tightly against her breast, the other picked up and shook the covers she and Troy had kicked off the bed sometime during the night. "I want my shirt. What did you do with it?"

"What did I..." He paused then began

again in a voice more controlled. "I didn't do anything with your shirt. *You're* the one who took it off."

Laura spun around in time to see the dimple disappear beneath the surface of his cheek. Her whole world had been destroyed in a single night, and he was laughing. "You think this is funny, don't you?"

He glanced away, took a deep breath then looked back. "No, Laura, I don't. But I sure don't think it's as serious as you're making it out to be, unless I'm missing something here." He raised a brow. "Am I, Laura? Am I missing something, because I sure as hell thought last night couldn't have been more perfect?"

"Last night was a mistake, Troy. It didn't change anything." She wiped a tear from her cheek. Last night *had* been perfect. The heat of their passion had slowly melted the coldness from around her heart and showed her how things should be, could be. But it had also fully awakened the dragon. "Nothing's changed from yesterday, do you hear?"

"Last night changed everything, and you can't run away from that fact."

"Go to hell."

With a quickness that startled her, Troy advanced on her until his face was within inches of her own. Though his eyes narrowed, his voice became dead calm. "The next time you tell me to go to hell, darlin', you'd better be prepared to come along for the ride."

Laura stood her ground, glare for glare. "For your information, *cowboy*, I've already been to hell, *and* I've got the scars to prove it!"

Nothing, no amount of wishing could put the words back into her mouth or silence their echo in the room. She watched his gaze sweep across the scar at her eyebrow, then drop to her chin. And Laura knew, as long as she lived, she'd never forget the look of pity to pass over his eyes.

'Where's your hero now, Laura?'

She backed away, putting distance between them. This time he didn't follow.

"Laura—"

"Don't." She shook her head. "What kind of example did I just set for Luke? Do you know how many talks I've had with him about the dangers of casual sex? I've even gone so far as to tell him to wait until marriage." Her tone was filled with self-derision.

"Then marry me, Laura."

His softly spoken words stunned her. "What?" she asked, not certain she'd heard correctly.

"I said marry me."

"I don't even know you."

"Last night wasn't a mistake."

"I–I" she stammered. "You seduced me."

"Seduced you?" His tone became incredulous. "How many times did I give you a chance to leave?"

'Whore's don't leave, do they, Laura?'

Shame pushed another rush of tears from her eyes, for those were Steve's favorite words to her. No matter how many times she'd threatened to leave him, she never did. She'd been too frightened to leave. She turned away and continued the search for her shirt.

"How many times, Laura?"

She wiped the tears but said nothing.

Troy continued. "What happened between us last night, in this room, wasn't something two people experience every day. Ask me, I know. And I know what I felt with you was real."

Laura straightened from checking for her

nightshirt under the bed. "What you felt?" She pitched the bulk of her long hair back over her shoulder and turned to face him. "What are you saying, Troy?" She spread her arm wide, while the other hand held the sheet tightly to her breast. "What? That you're in love with me?"

Hearing the words aloud seemed to stop him for a moment.

He shrugged his shoulder. "Yeah, that's what I'm saying."

She could hear Steve laughing.

She couldn't tell if the look in Troy's eyes was sadness or regret. His apparent indifference to the fact hurt. She choked back a sob. "And just how many times did you say you loved me last night?" Her voice rose steadily louder with each word. She watched his expression go blank.

"How many times, Troy? Oh, wait, maybe you whispered the words in my ear, and I just didn't hear you. Is that it? Did you whisper them to me, Troy?"

Finding old habits hard to break, she sought to hide her emotions behind the wall of ice. But the wall wasn't there, and her words echoed with his continued silence.

"Goddamn it, answer me." Her tears were

falling too fast to keep wiped away, so she allowed them to fall freely. "Well, I'll tell you. None! That's how many." Then she pointed at the bed. "Do you think it was love we made in that bed?"

'What's he know about loving a whore?'

Troy took a deep breath and raked his hand through his hair. The look in his eyes wretched her heart. "It *was* for me, Laura. If it wasn't for you then tell me what you need to make it so, and if it's within my power, I'll give it to you."

'Go on, Laura. Tell him you like your loving rough, the way I used to make you beg it from me.'

Laura turned away before Troy saw how deep her own pain went. She wanted dreams without nightmares. Until then, she knew she couldn't return the love. Steve had made sure of that.

Angry with Steve and angry at her inability to forget, Laura kicked the sheet away so she could move. She stopped and looked up through her tears. "Sex doesn't make love. You can't *make* love, Troy. It has to grow. And we don't know enough about each other for anything..." Her sentence broke with a gasp. Her gaze moved passed him and caught the reflection of his back in the mirror behind him, unable to believe what she saw. She stared down at her fingernails. Slowly she returned her gaze to his.

Troy frowned before glancing over his shoulder into the mirror. The skin hadn't been broken, but the long scratches across his back shoulders told their own story.

He worked himself around to get a better look then threw her a proud grin. "Believe me, honey, you made those by letting go, not holding on."

"Ooooh!" Laura reached down, and with her free hand, she pulled the sheet up from around her feet and stomped toward the door.

"Blue," he said.

She looked back over her shoulder. "What?"

"My favorite color is blue. And my favorite day of the week is Saturday. My favorite food—"

He's lost his mind. "What are you talking about?"

"You said we hardly know each other and love has to grow, right?"

Laura nodded, still uncertain.

"Well, princess, I'm just planting a few

seeds."

'You're not a princess, never were, never will be. Once a tramp, always a tramp.'

Laura closed her eyes and felt one more tear squeeze through her lashes. How could she tell him that last night was a dream? How could she tell him even though the wall of ice had melted and softened the soil, the weeds Steve had planted needed to be destroyed before anything else could grow? The evil dragon had to be destroyed—

'It'll never happen, baby,' Steve's voice taunted.

Placing a trembling hand on the doorknob, Laura opened the door and walked blindly out into the hall with the extra length of sheet trailing behind her.

"Laura, wait," Troy called, scrambling after her. Suddenly there was a loud thump, followed by a mumbled curse.

She looked back. He'd stubbed his toe on the dresser. She smiled, feeling little solace for his pain.

"Here," he said, limping toward the doorway. He held out her nightshirt. Her eyes widened. She reached out for it, but he quickly pulled it back. "Not even if you wished for the moon. But," he paused with a raised eyebrow. "Maybe, if you wished on a star."

Slowly his words mixed with memories: 'You smell like a wish come true' and something to do with her hair.

Her teary eyes narrowed. "Is that what happened in there last night?" She indicated the room with an upward thrust of her chin. "Is that all I was? A wish on a falling star?" She grabbed a handful of her unbound hair and held it out. "This too?"

The pain in her chest became so great she could hardly breathe. The star had been after all, not for her. She shook her head, forcing her voice past the suffocating lump in her throat. "I just wanted a knight in shining armor."

Troy laid his palm against her cheek, his thumb brushing away the wetness. "Fairytales, princess? Sorry. All I can offer is a flesh and blood man."

'What? No hero, no knight in shining armor?' Steve's voice mocked.

Laura felt lightheaded. For a moment she thought she would collapse. Suddenly it wasn't

Troy standing before her with her nightshirt. It was Steve, standing over her, wrapping his tee-shirt around his fist as she scrambled to the far side of their bed.

"Laura..."

She focused on Troy's eyes. Was it love or pity she saw? She wasn't sure of anything right now. Breaking away she turned toward her room but stopped abruptly.

Four faces were watching from the top of the stairs.

Troy stepped into the hall. She glanced back. Was he coming after her? She wouldn't know for sure, for he too had stopped short when he noticed the audience.

Unable to hold back her cry of sorrow, Laura ran to her room, slamming the door shut behind her. Then just as quickly, she opened the door and yanked the trailing end of the sheet into the room with her, slamming the door shut again. A few moments later she heard Troy's door shut just as loudly.

Laura cried. She felt as if her heart was actually breaking in two, releasing an unending supply of tears.

Toward evening, Rebecca came up and told her Troy had gone back to Denver. Burying her face in her pillow, Laura cried harder.

Sleep finally came out of sheer exhaustion, but even in sleep she found no peace. In her dream, Troy rode the black stallion in circles around her, slowly working her towards the edge of a rocky cliff.

At the cliff's edge, he leaned down and scooped her up to him. For several moments, he gazed down into her eyes. He lowered his mouth to hers, his kiss slow and purposeful. And that purpose, she realized too late, was to draw the love she had hidden from him to the surface of her eyes. Yet before she could open them and let him see, he let her slip from his grasp.

Into the dark deep cavern she fell. Tumbling blindly in pitch-blackness.

Is this what love is like, free falling in the dark?

Then, through the fear and uncertainty of falling, her heart released an overwhelming pang. Would he be there, waiting to catch her when she reached the bottom?

CHAPTER TEN

LAURA SCANNED the lower shelves in the boutique's small stockroom for the third time for the customer order she was attempting to locate. This was so not like her. *Focus, Laura, focus.* But focusing had become difficult of late.

And getting back into her normal routine had become even harder. Damn near impossible, in fact.

In the two weeks she'd been back from vacation all she seemed able to think about was the night she'd spent with Troy. And the fact that he'd called everyday of those two weeks wasn't helping.

So far she'd managed to avoid talking to him, usually by letting the answering machine at home catch the call or instructing the employees at the boutique to say she wasn't there. It had become a vicious cycle of hide-n-seek.

Her dreams at night bounced between nightmares of Steve out to hurt her and Troy out to rescue her. She always woke feeling tired, rundown. And then this morning she woke up feeling nauseous.

What on earth was she going to do about that man?

She pulled a package from the shelf and looked at the label. She shoved it back realizing she'd misread the name. So help her, if she miss-filled one more order, she swore she was going to have to fire herself.

Her eyes continued their search of the packages on the top shelf. She stopped. *There it is.* She sighed heavily. *Figures.* She'd need the ladder.

She dragged the ladder over, but as soon as she positioned it in place, her thoughts returned to Troy. Why didn't he take the hint and leave her alone, count her on his list of broken hearts? If he had a list.

The ladder rocked unevenly as she began her upward accent. Of course he had a list. Every man had a list. And that's all he was, a man, nothing special.

She was halfway up the ladder when she heard someone at the doorway clear her throat. Laura glanced over her shoulder and saw Sandy. The ladder rocked.

"Sorry to bother you, Laura, but there's a customer at the counter insisting on talking with you."

"See if Donna can deal with it. I'm having my own problems." The ladder wobbled, proving her point.

"Okay, I'll get her, but you were specifically asked for." Sandy walked out.

Laura turned her attention back to the task at hand. She stepped on the top rung and reached up with one hand. *Almost.* She eased onto her tiptoes and stretched again, this time able to work the package forward with her fingertips.

The wooden structure beneath her rocked precariously. Her heart lodged in her throat. She shut her eyes, but not before she saw her life flash before them. It might not have been much of a life to others, but it was hers, and damn if she didn't want to keep living it.

Behind her, at the doorway she heard a sound. Without taking her attention off the three packages balanced in the palm of her hand, she snapped, "All right, Sandy, I'll be out in a minute."

"A minute, an hour, makes no difference,

Laura. I'll wait for as long as it takes."

Troy! Startled, the boxes in her hand pitched into the air. She reached out to grab them. Too late. She felt her body twisting.

Her hand brushed across several rows of boxed orders and knocked them from the shelf. Like packed parachutes, the lids burst open spilling their contents of silk and satin into the air. Her right foot slipped from the step and she felt herself teeter out into mid-air.

Out the corner of her eye she saw Troy bolt from the doorway, his black duster billowing out behind him like the wings of an angel.

Laura cried out as she fell from the ladder.

Troy caught her against him with one arm. Yet the scattered layers of lace and satin on the floor had him skating about until his left foot slipped out from underneath him and sent him backward to the floor.

Laura squeezed her eyes shut. *Not again!*

A moment later, Laura found herself lying on top of him. She looked into his eyes, her heart pounding. "You saved my life."

"You nearly scared me to death." His eyes sparkled with humor. "Though I must say, I'm getting real used to you being on top."

It only took a second for his comment to penetrate the thick fog of shock. "Ohhhh!" Her cheeks burned. She scrambled off him, ignoring his low grunt of discomfort as her knee pressed against his groin.

"What are you doing here?" she demanded as she stood and brushed at her skirt.

He sat up. "You don't answer your phone. Are you purposely ignoring my calls?"

"I've-I've been busy."

Troy remained sitting on the floor. He drew a knee up, resting his right arm across it. He held his left arm, still supported by the sling, against his abdomen. Discomfort shadowed his features. "I need a housekeeper."

Guilt made her look away. "I'm *very* busy." She'd hoped he'd forgotten the bet. He hadn't. She was a nervous wreck from just thinking about him, dreaming about him. How could she clean for him? Spend hours with him underfoot, smelling him, hearing his voice. Remembering their night together? She couldn't. The evil dragon had settled down, and she wasn't about to stir him again.

"I can't make it," she said. Stooping, she

busied herself gathering lingerie that had spilled from the boxes.

He rose to his haunches to help her. "When, this week? Next?"

"Never," she answered, purposely avoiding eye contact. The scent of his cologne wafted past her nose, filling her mind with vivid memories of how he'd looked at her during their night together.

"Funny," he said.

"What's funny?"

"Lingerie."

"What's so funny about it?"

"Women, placing so much importance on what they wear to bed for a man when the end result is to be wearing nothing at all."

"I heard a scream." A familiar voice came from the doorway. "Ohmigosh, what happened? Are you two all right?"

Laura glanced up. Donna stood in the doorway with a look of disbelief on her face. Thankful for the interruption from Troy's line of questioning and intruding memories, Laura stuffed a matching set of silk and satin into the box beside her. "I thought you were going to replace the ladder while I was on vacation?"

"Wow, Laura, who's your friend?" Donna asked.

Laura cringed inwardly. Her best friend's transformation into Stupid Cupid had begun.

Seeing herself between a rock and a hard spot, Laura debated how best to introduce Troy, but before she could open her mouth, he stood and extended his hand.

"Troy Hawke. You must be Donna."

Looking him up and down, Donna nodded.

Troy returned to his haunches. "Laura talked quite a bit about you while we were on vacation." He reached for an empty box.

Laura almost choked. His 'while *we* were on vacation', made it sound intimate. She slanted him a glance just in time to catch sight of the dimple in his cheek fade beneath the surface. Memories of his emergency room visit told her she had to stop him from talking. "He's Rebecca's brother. He *tagged* along on vacation."

Donna knelt down beside him and reached out for a box. Her lips turned up in a smile Laura thought looked more like Cupid's bow being drawn, ready to fire. "You and Laura get snowed in at the townhouse?"

"We didn't get snowed in," Laura quickly corrected, stuffing a red lace teddy into the box in her hand.

"Well..." Troy scooped up several pair of green satin panties. He looked at Laura, his eyes flashing with laughter. "It *did* snow quite a bit." Gently he placed the panties into the box in front of him.

"But we weren't snowed in," Laura stated emphatically. She reached out and grabbed a pair of black stockings.

"Did you injure your arm skiing?" Donna held out a forest green satin bra toward his arm, indicating the cast.

Troy shrugged, took the bra, and added it to the box with the panties. "I took a little tumble down the hill."

Jamming more stockings and panties into the box in her hand, Laura looked at him and frowned. A little tumble? He'd been a hero. Why was he downplaying what had happened? *A hero.* A rush of warmth filled her. "He jumped off the ski lift to save a woman after her drunken boyfriend pushed her off."

Donna gasped and put a hand to the base of her throat. She looked at Troy. "Seriously, you

Keeper of the Stars

jumped?"

"It wasn't *that* far of a drop." He cast a scowling glance at Laura.

Laura sensed his discomfort, almost to the point of embarrassment. Suddenly it dawned on her. He didn't do what he did to be recognized or honored. He played the hero because that's the stuff he was made of.

"So you got hurt when you jumped?" Donna asked.

Laura shook her head and answered for him. "It was after he jumped, when he was helping the injured woman. Her creep of a boyfriend skied down and plowed right into him."

"Laura was the great one though," Troy said, and the subtle change in his gray eyes warned Laura his humorous mood had returned. "After we got back to the townhouse, she stayed the night in my room making sure I didn't doze off with the concussion I'd received. She didn't leave my side until morning." His dimpled smile lit up the room. "She plays nursemaid very well." He held out his hand toward Laura. A black thong dangled from his fingertip.

"She spent the *entire* night with you?"

Donna asked incredulously.

Laura snatched the thong from Troy's hand. Their knuckles grazed. Each pulled their hand back quickly. The thong dropped to the floor. Their gaze met and locked. Laura was sure he could hear her wildly beating heart relaying her feelings of love.

He scowled.

The look had the effect of water doused on fire. Laura stood quickly, not wanting him to see the pain in her eyes. She reached over Troy and grabbed Donna by the upper arm and dragged her to her feet. Placing a hand at her friend's back, Laura pushed her toward the door. "I have a mess to clean up in here, and since you're running your mouth more than helping, go tell Charlotte she'll have to wait a while longer for her order—"

"Wait." Donna deftly rolled away from Laura's hand and faced Troy again. "He didn't get a chance to answer my question." She walked back and stooped down beside him. "Laura actually spent the night with you?"

"Yep, couldn't get her to leave my side. But now..." He exaggerated a deep sign. "Now that I've come to collect on a bet we made... " He shrugged his shoulder before carefully tucking the edges of a satin nightshirt down into another box.

"Bet? What bet? Pray tell." Donna took the box from him and closed the lid.

"It's nothing, Donna, really," Laura said between clenched teeth.

"I can't seem to recall at the moment what we bet on. Can you, Laura?" He looked at her.

Butterflies beat the rhythm of the words in her stomach. *Control. A lover's kiss, for ten seconds.* "It slips my mind at the moment." Her eyes pleaded for mercy.

"Anyway," Troy continued. "Laura lost the bet. She agreed to clean house for me once a week until I healed. But now she tells me she's too busy."

"*What?*" Donna shot to her feet and spun on Laura. "How could you do that to him? And after him risking his life to save someone?" She glanced down at Troy and crooned, "Poor darling." She smiled back at Laura. Laura was certain she had just been placed in the bulls-eye of Cupid's target. "It's settled then. The girls and I can take care of the shop while you finish taking care of him."

Laura opened her mouth to argue, but

instead bent a seething glare on Troy. "Perhaps I can make it next Thursday."

"Perhaps?" His dimple appeared.

She huffed. "Just call me with the time."

He held up several more thongs for her to take, and though the dimple remained, his smile didn't quite reach his eyes this time. "Next Thursday will be fine."

After Laura carefully extracted the thongs from his hand, he stood and touched the brim of his cowboy hat with his forefinger. "It was a real pleasure to meet you, Donna." Turning, he left the stockroom.

Donna moved to the doorway and watched him leave. "Wow."

Laura sneaked a peek over Donna's shoulder.

He strolled with confidence and ease toward the front door and touched his forefinger to the brim of his hat at a group of women standing at the counter. "Ladies."

As if their movements had been choreographed, the women returned his goodbye, turned their heads to watch him leave then sighed in unison.

Donna turned and Laura took a quick step

back to avoid getting bumped. She fidgeted under Donna's glare.

"Now that," Donna pointed out the stockroom door, "is what you call a knight in shining armor. And a damn good smelling one, too!"

CHAPTER ELEVEN

"THE MAN'S RELENTLESS, incorrigible!"

Laura whipped her SUV in beside Troy's black Chevy truck.

Two weeks had passed since his unexpected visit to the boutique. She hadn't made it to clean for him the week before. Truth was she'd started feeling sick in the mornings. She'd stayed home from the boutique and away from Donna for several days until finally on Thursday she'd gone to see the doctor.

A lover's kiss, for ten seconds. If it'd only stayed that simple. But it hadn't, and her life would never be the same because of it.

Thursday afternoon, when she didn't call or show, Troy had left a message in that hypnotically smooth voice of his. "Laura, this is Troy. If you don't return my calls this time, I'll make another visit to the boutique. This time it won't be pretty."

She hadn't thought the last time was pretty.

Though his voice evoked memories of a

night of passion, his words definitely did not. Within five minutes, she was returning his call.

"What happened?" he'd asked.

"I've been sick."

"Can you make it next week?"

No, never. "I promise, next week."

She'd given in and now, here she was in front of his house with a heart racing so fast she could give the best Indy drivers a run for their money.

Laura looked up at his house and released a groan of despair. It was easily three times the size of her own house, and she knew how long that took to clean. Glancing at her watch, she supposed she'd have to cancel her shopping plans for the afternoon.

She was by no means a doctor, but surely his injuries had healed well enough in the last four weeks for him to clean his own house or call someone in from the Jolly Dolly Maid Service. Heck, they'd probably even wear a French maid uniform for him.

'Be here by eight' had sounded too much like an order. She didn't take orders from any man, not any more. So she'd waited until ten o'clock before

leaving her house, though an earlier bout with morning sickness wouldn't have allowed her to be here any sooner.

Unable to put off the inevitable any longer, she sighed heavily, opened the door of her SUV and climbed out. She reached back inside for her heavy jacket. The forecast had called for flurries. This time she came prepared.

Shaky legs carried her up the walk to the front porch. She rang the bell and waited, holding a hand against her stomach. *Damn butterflies!* She'd had three whole days since his last call to prepare for this moment, but now the moment had arrived and she wasn't ready. Not even close.

What would they say to each other? What if he reached out and gathered her in his arms, what then?

Laura glanced at her SUV.

She would do the only thing she knew how to do. Run.

The bet wasn't a contract or anything legally binding. She cast another contemplating glance toward her vehicle. There was nothing stopping her from turning around and leaving. To hell with the bet. She stepped back.

The door opened. She looked up.

Keeper of the Stars

There he stood, larger and more real than anything her memories had teased her with. And only Heaven knew, how many times in the last two weeks she'd spent remembering.

The thatch of black hair fell carelessly over his forehead giving him that sexy, devil-may-care look. And if the pleasure her eyes received from looking at him wasn't a sin, then the thoughts to follow certainly were.

Apart from his tie being loosened and the absence of a suit jacket, he looked dressed for a day at the office. A crisp white shirt tucked into dark suit pants complimented his dark looks and trim length.

Her focus moved to his eyes. There her mental affirmations of him came to an abrupt halt. Though his eyes were bright and clear, the scowl that dipped his brows together seemed to forecast an impending storm.

He brought his wrist up and gave his watch a pointed glance. "You're late."

A prick of conscience made her look away. Well, so much for being gathered in his arms. "I'm only here to do a little cleaning, why does it matter what time I show?"

His scowl darkened as he stepped aside. Though she doubted he would say the words himself, the scent of his cologne, as it wafted past her nose, welcomed her in.

How she'd missed that scent.

She resisted the urge to inhale a deep dose of him. One that would last a lifetime. The last thing she needed today was to get caught up in his spells and potions. Perhaps it would be wise to hold her breath until she was a safe distance past him. And if she passed out from lack of oxygen, maybe he'd take pity and send her home.

She stepped inside. "Were you going somewhere?"

The muscle at the back of his jaw flexed. "I had to be at a meeting for my dad at nine, but since you hadn't showed or called to let me know you were running late, I had to cancel, and that in turn cancelled the entire meeting."

Laura glanced away. She didn't want to cause him trouble at his father's office. She just wanted him to call off the bet. "Well, I'm here now." And the sooner she got started the sooner she could be out of there.

"You can start by hanging your coat in the closet then follow me." He turned and closed the front door with a resounding click.

Laura followed, trying to keep her gaze from constantly straying to his cute little backside. A backside she remembered...

Laura stopped herself. She couldn't allow herself to remember. Remembering would rouse the evil dragon, and as she'd found out long ago, he lived in her memories, along with her dreams, wishes, needs and desires. If she stirred up one, she stirred up the other. Heaven help her, but it was going to make for a very long day if she didn't practice a little thought control.

"You have a very nice... house." She closed her eyes, swallowed hard and quickly added *no looking* to her growing list of *no touching* and *no smelling*.

"I'll tell my father you said so."

"Your father?"

"This is his house, I live in Montana, remember?" he replied. Not breaking stride, he headed toward the swinging door on the other side of a large dining room.

With his words, Laura remembered the reason Rebecca had told her Troy was in Denver. To help run the office of their father's company until he recuperated from back surgery. "How is your father doing?"

Before the swinging door of the kitchen, Troy stopped and turned around. "He's doing fine. After the surgery was cancelled and rescheduled twice, he's glad it's finally over. He'll be home next week."

"Talking about home, I imagine you're anxious to get back to Montana." Back to Montana, far away from her.

Troy placed his hand against the swinging door and smiled, making no comment, but sticking to business. "Perhaps the kitchen would be a good place to start your cleaning." He pushed and held open the door.

The sight greeting her nearly made her turn around and run. The room was a disaster area! Never in her life had she seen a kitchen in such a state, even after Luke's cooking experiments.

Pots, pans, and dishes were piled high in the sink and on the counter. The dishwasher door hung open, and that too was overflowing with dirty dishes.

Footprints, tracking in all directions across the tile floor could almost have passed for steps that had been laid down to teach some newfangled hip-hop dance, except these had been laid out in mud, dried mud. Then there was an odd smell that quickly overpowered the trailing scent of his cologne.

"Ohmigod! What happened?" The words spewed forth before she could stop them. She took several steps into the kitchen then turned to face him.

"Funny you should ask." He leaned against the doorframe. "There was this lady who agreed...if she lost a bet...to come by once a week to clean up until my shoulder and ribs healed. I started calling her, hoping to set up arrangements, but she wouldn't return my calls. Over the week that followed, I managed, with some discomfort, to cook and clean myself."

Laura felt the warmth of a flush moving up her neck with each word.

"Along about Monday of this week," he continued, "movement to my shoulder had become restricted from doing all this work myself. So weighing my choices, I had to let the place go until the lady showed." He paused, indicating with a slight thrust of his chin. "Though I think the trash is starting to become a problem."

Laura looked in the direction of the trashcan overflowing with an assortment of frozen TV dinner boxes. As she looked, a box, balanced precariously on top of the pile, suddenly slipped off and hit the floor, triggering a chain reaction of the others.

She had hoped by ignoring his phone calls, he'd just quit calling and give up on her, but once again she had underestimated him. Unable to hide her disbelief, Laura faced him. "Why didn't you call a cleaning service?"

"*We* had a bet."

"It's going to take me hours to clean up this mess!"

A smile tugged at the corner of his mouth. "Then I suggest you get started. You're already two hours behind schedule."

"Y-you..." she stammered. "You did this on purpose."

"You should have returned my calls." He leveled his iron gray gaze on her.

"It was a stupid bet." She stomped her foot on the floor.

He arched a black brow at her tantrum. "Why? Because you lost?"

She pressed her lips together and glanced

away.

"I thought so."

Still avoiding his gaze, she flitted her hand about. "Winning, losing, makes no difference. You could have controlled this."

"You're mad because I'm holding you to your word."

Resenting his perceptiveness, she glared at him. "We both know you got more than was bargained for with that bet. Why can't we just call it even?"

"Because what happened between us *after* you came into my room has nothing to do with the bet."

'You lost that bet because you're a tramp, Laura.' Steve's words settled as a mere whisper in the back of her mind, and Laura's heart grew heavy with dread, for the evil dragon had awoken.

Now was the time to run. She stepped forward intending to brush past him, but he straightened and blocked her path of escape. She stopped short of running into his chest and looked up into his eyes. She opened her mouth to demand he step aside, but he reached up and put his forefinger against her lips.

"Do you really want to discuss just why you lost that bet?" he asked quietly, searching her eyes.

In the instant he touched her, the power of their attraction vibrated through her like the aftershock of an earthquake, weakening her determination to stay in control and crumbling her will to say no.

She knew she should keep herself safely at arm's length from him, but she found it hard when the need to be held safely within his arms was stronger.

He cupped her chin, lightly brushing the pad of his thumb across her lips. Held captive in the warmth of his gaze, she watched helplessly as he lowered his head. At the last moment, he hesitated, long enough for her to say no.

And of course, she was going to say no, she told herself. She was going to say no and then...then she closed her eyes and felt his mouth settle on her lips, dissolving her 'no' into a long blissful sigh.

Her body recognized his scent, his touch, his taste, and she found her mind wanting to follow in the celebration. She allowed her tongue to trace the line between his closed lips, beckoning him to open and let her in, only to whimper like a spoiled child when he refused.

He pressed his lips to the corner of her mouth before moving on to her ear. She was melting against him, kiss by kiss and it was the most wonderful feeling, and for a moment she managed to keep Steve's taunting whispers away.

"Laura?"

"Hmmm?"

"The cleaning supplies are under the sink."

Like a train on a rickety track, her mind jostled his words about until they hit a smooth stretch and registered. When they did, they affected her like a train wreck.

"Ohhh!" She brought her hands up and pushed against his chest. Taking a step back she glared at him.

He tapped his watch. "If I were you I wouldn't waste any more time."

CHAPTER TWELVE

LAURA SCRUBBED, rinsed, and mopped until at last, the kitchen glowed. Her shirt was damp and clingy. Finally, unable to bear it any longer, she unbuttoned her shirt as far as she dared. Though she hadn't seen Troy since she sent the kitchen door bumping against his backside, she knew better than to let her guard down completely.

Standing in front of the sink, she placed her hands on her hips and surveyed the kitchen. It'd taken two hours, but she was done, thanks in part to a little elbow grease fueled in turn by a good portion of indignation.

She tore a paper towel from the roll, ran it under the faucet and patted her neck with it. Next, she pulled a glass from the cabinet.

After finishing the last drop of water with a sigh, she stood for several moments with her eyes closed and her head tipped back. To be still, felt too good for words. She'd worked out her frustration and now felt relaxed.

The quiet creaking of a door prickled the hairs at the back of her neck. She opened one eye in the direction of the swinging door.

Troy stood watching her. There was no mistaking the look in his gray eyes. She'd seen it too many times during their night together.

With a trembling hand, Laura set the glass on the counter and turned her back to him. She fumbled nervously with the buttons on her shirt. Heat filled her cheeks, remembering what had followed that look in his eyes.

She dragged the back of her hand along her temple in an attempt to lay into submission the few strands of hair that had come loose from her braid. Pausing, she pulled in a deep breath before turning to face him.

His eyes scanned the kitchen.

She held her breath.

The look he settled on her had changed to one of genuine surprise. "Wow," was all he said.

She exhaled. Just that one simple word from him swelled her heart with a long needed dose of self-worth. It shouldn't have mattered what he thought, but it did.

She tossed the paper towel into the trash. "What's next?"

His eyes took on a glimmering shine that she had also seen before. One of challenge. He smiled. "Laundry."

Laura grimaced. She'd rather do windows.

His smile drew her attention to his mouth. She knew better than to argue or reply with some sarcastic comment. His manner of silencing her proved to be more than her heart could handle.

"There's a load of towels. No underwear, in case that's what your look of panic was about."

"I wasn't panicking."

"Good." His smile widened. "Then my bed sheets need washed too."

Now she panicked. Before she could mention something about windows, he tossed her a key. "It's a spare I had made for you. Keep it. I have to leave for a short while. When you finish just lock up on your way out.

Laura stared at the key in her hand. She tried to hide her sudden feeling of disappointment behind a look of relief. "You're leaving?"

"I might not be back before five. If you can think of anything else to keep you here until then, stay. If not then..." He left the sentence unfinished.

Anything else to keep her here? She could think of plenty to keep her here. Captivating gray eyes, a dimpled smile, the touch of his hand that had her absolutely melting in his palm. But what was he saying?

Hope clutched at her heart.

'Poor Laura, always hoping, always wishing. Always happy to be the whore.'

Steve's cruel words caught her off guard and hit hard. Breath caught painfully in her chest.

'Look at him, Laura. Do you really think he wants you to stay because he loves you? What fairytale world are you living in to believe he would want someone like you?'

"Laura, are you feeling okay?" Troy took a hesitant step toward her.

Finding it hard to swallow past the burning lump in her throat, Laura turned and busied herself with folding a dish towel. "I'll be gone before you return." Several moments passed before she heard him walk away.

Later, having pulled herself together enough to focus on the task at hand, Laura finally took a few minutes to grab a bite to eat. Seated on a barstool at the island counter in the kitchen with a sandwich, Laura thought of all the TV dinner boxes she'd thrown out. How long had it been since he'd had a real stove-cooked meal?

Compassion filled her. He'd only been injured in the first place because he'd tried to save someone. And as for the bet, she knew the conditions if she'd lost.

Fixing him dinner wasn't part of the deal, and he might not even notice, but the thought of doing it for him stoked a fire and filled her with wonderful warmth.

Jumping up from the stool, she began her search through the freezer and pantry for the things she needed.

A half hour later, satisfied with her choice of menu, Laura found herself outside Troy's bedroom door. She took a deep breath, turned the knob and walked in.

Like a kid in a candy store allowed only to touch and smell, her senses kicked into overdrive. She opened his dresser drawers. Her fingers touched his boxers and cotton undershirts, folded and tucked with attention to detail. She found his scent in a bottle of his cologne and on a deep red Dakota shirt he'd hung in his closet. Desire became an ache within her breasts. Could he be her knight in shining armor?

'There's no such thing.'

Laura squeezed her eyes shut in an attempt to push out Steve's voice. She would prove him wrong, she had too. After a moment she took a deep breath, collected herself and continued on.

She fingered Troy's gold cuff links and tiepins in a dish upon his dresser. She trailed her long fingernails across several pairs of Wranglers in the closet. He was a cowboy. He was a businessman. But without a doubt she could testify, beneath the layers of clothing, he was all man.

Laura shut the closet door. She glanced across the room to the unmade bed. Her thoughts shifted from searching for her knight to remembering a night she would never forget.

The thought of his dimpled smile gave her a heady feeling. His gray eyes, when they sparkled with laughter, made her happy. But above all, she remembered his kisses bringing her back to life.

Forcing the memory aside before it sidetracked her from her duties, Laura reached down and pulled the comforter back.

After running the bundle of linen to the washer, she pulled the new set of sheets out of the hall closet. They touched her cheek. Their clean, fresh smell made her aware of her own grungy condition.

She made the bed, brushing her hand over the foot of the comforter as a final touch to her housecleaning duties. Turning, Laura surveyed the room.

She glanced at the clock. He would be home soon. She would be gone by then. A sinking feeling washed over her. Wearily, she brushed the back of her hand against her temple trying to control a loose stand of hair.

Pausing, she glanced at Troy's bathroom, which had been spotless to begin with. Her glance returned to the clock on the nightstand.

To hell with it, she was going to leave the same way she arrived. Washed, refreshed and in clean clothes.

***

"No, Troy, she hasn't been home or called." Luke's voice carried through the ear piece secured around Troy's ear.

Troy looked into the rearview mirror seeing nothing but a swirling white world behind him. The day's forecasted flurries had turned into a full-blown winter storm.

The emergency crew closed the road behind him, and he knew he was lucky to have made it this far. Yet his thoughts were not so much on himself as they were on Laura and how she faired on her drive home.

"Call me as soon as you hear from her or have her call as soon as she gets in," Troy instructed.

"I hope nothing's happened. It's pretty bad out there."

The note of worry in Luke's voice struck a nerve, and though he wouldn't admit it out loud, that had been his exact thought when he'd been unable to reach her at his dad's house. Then he'd tried ringing her house, not reaching Luke until the third try.

"Most likely she stopped off somewhere on her way home," Troy tried to reassure Luke. But the assurance sounded hollow. "Just try not to leave the house until you hear from her or me again, okay?"

Amy Lynn

"Okay."

Troy ended the call and scrolled through numbers on his cell phone until he found the boutique's number. Maybe, just maybe she stopped by there on her way home. After four rings it was answered by a pre-recorded message, *"...regular hours of business are..."*

"Damn it, Laura, where are you?" He pitched the phone onto the passenger seat.

If anything had happened to her, he'd never forgive himself. He never should have left the house today. He should have just stayed out of her way. Hell, he should have just solved his problem by taking a long, cold shower.

The weeks following his return from Breckenridge had been hell. She'd avoided his calls, making it perfectly clear she wanted nothing more to do with him. Though he'd never intended to hold her to the bet, it'd been all he'd had to connect her to him.

When he opened his door to her standing on the front porch this morning, his first impulse was to reach out and wrap her in his arms. But she would have fought and run. He didn't want to chance that mistake again. He promised himself he'd pretend indifference.

Keeper of the Stars

He found himself almost breaking that promise when he saw her in the kitchen drawing the wet paper towel across her throat. He hadn't been able to look away from the open neckline of her shirt where the swell of her breast glistened with moisture.

He'd summoned up all the control he had not to go to her and rip her shirt the rest of the way open and bury his face into the valley between. Even now, the beat of his heart echoed the sound of shirt buttons popping off and bouncing on the tile floor.

Just one thorough kiss would have had her melting against him. There would have been nothing to stop him from wrapping his hands around her waist and lifting her up onto the sparkling clean kitchen counter top to finish what he'd started.

There would have been nothing to stop him except the fear beneath the surface of her eyes.

Leaving today had been the right decision.

Troy peered through the quickly freezing snow on his windshield. With the power outage, the neighborhood took on the appearance of something out of a Steven King novel.

Amy Lynn

He spotted his driveway. He was home now and Laura was...*still here?*

A small piece of worry broke loose and transformed itself into pleasant surprise as he pulled in beside her now snow-buried SUV.

A power outage? Dusk approaching? The only road out now closed? The domino effect of events ended with one fact. There was no chance in hell of her leaving. Not tonight. A spark of hope teased a smile from his lips.

Troy killed the engine. If the power returned tonight, he'd come back out and put their vehicles into the garage. Right now his focus was on finding out what had kept her here.

There hadn't been that much to clean. The kitchen had been the worst of it, and it had taken him most of the night to get it looking that way.

He unlocked the front door and kicked his feet against the step before entering. The house was cloaked in eerie silence. *Where was she?* He paused to listen.

Silence. Dead eerie silence.

Then he sniffed. The house was...mouth-wateringly delicious?

He passed through the living room. The heavy drapes blocked out the last remaining light of day. The house felt cold and empty.

"Laura!" he called out. He turned his head, catching a faint sound in the direction of the kitchen. "Laura!" This time with more urgency.

"I-I'm in here, Troy. In the...in the kitchen."

His heightened senses picked up on a note of panic in her voice, triggering new concerns that she might have injured herself in some way.

He reached the kitchen and with one hand pushed open the door without breaking stride. "Laura, are you..?"

He was no more than three steps into the kitchen when the scene before him brought him to an abrupt halt and rendered him speechless.

In less than a second, his gaze swept across the kitchen. But it wasn't the lit candles on the counter top that held his attention, nor the one she was working to light now.

Nor was it the reflecting surface of the island counter where laid out was a fare fit for a king. Stuffed pork chops, mashed potatoes, dinner rolls, a vegetable and salad.

Even still, the aroma of the home-cooked meal wasn't enough to hold his awakened senses. Something deep inside and, everything he was as a man, focused on Laura.

She stood at the counter. With a hand that trembled, she attempted to light the candle before her. The match dropped from her fingers before the wick caught. She tore off another and scratched it across the dark band of the matchbook. The sudden flash of fire threw her shadow onto the wall behind her. As the flame on the match tip died down, the burning wick of the candle cast a soft golden halo about her unbound hair and...

"Laura, where are your clothes?"

CHAPTER THIRTEEN

LAURA DROPPED the match and looked up. Her eyes were green, wide and full of uncertainty. The flame on the candle flickered at the touch of her breath.

He stood, not trusting himself to move yet feeling the need to loosen the knot of his tie so he could breathe easier. It wouldn't be hard to imagine how she'd spent the rest of her afternoon in his kitchen. Mixing up potions and conjuring up some spell to drive him crazy with desire.

He looked at her. One thought repeated itself over and over in his mind: *He'd died and gone to heaven...*

"My clothes?" There was a slight inflection in her voice. Her hand drew together the collar of the shirt she was wearing, *his* favorite deep red Dakota shirt. "Actually, they're in the washing machine."

"All your clothes?" He forced himself to keep talking. Keeping a conversation going would hopefully lessen the chance of his imagination running rampant or anything else from happening.

Her mouth did the familiar fish out of water routine before she answered. "Yes, everything..." her voice trailed away.

Oh God, he'd had to ask. And of course he had to look. The shirttail came to a V, touching her legs mid-thigh, and at the sides near her hip, it was bare.

Her confession lit the fuse to his imagination, exploding it wide open. He squeezed his eyes shut and swore silently.

"Hey, look. I'm sorry, okay," she huffed, apparently mistaking his agitation. "I felt so grungy after cleaning, I-I took a shower, then I just couldn't stand the thought of climbing back into my dirty clothes, and I was going to be dressed and gone before you got back."

And on she went with her reasons and explanations. As she rambled on, his brain stuck on the, I took a shower, thing.

Damn, damn, damn. He squeezed his eyes shut again. She'd been in his shower naked and wet. His imagination latched onto a water droplet, and like a brush stroke, his mind's eye followed it down her throat and between her breast where it rode over her abdomen and around her navel losing itself from his view in the soft golden curls between her...

"...and I know how bad you wanted me gone before you came back home."

Her last comment knocked over the wonderful picture in his mind and brought him back to the real world. He frowned. *Wanted her gone?* If anything, he wanted to tell her she was welcome to stay forever. Only right now he had to tell her about the road closures. "Laura—"

"I would have been gone too, but the power went out before the wash cycle was completed."

Thank you, Mother Nature!

"I didn't know what else to do, so I borrowed one of your shirts." She threw her arms wide to prove the fact and the cuffs fell over her hands with a good length to spare. She sighed and bunched the sleeves back over her forearms.

"I need to call Luke. Your phone doesn't work. My cell phone is in the SUV."

"Laura—"

"I hate to ask, but if you could lend me a pair of sweats and some socks to wear home, I'll return them when I come back next week and—"

"Laura, you can't go."

She blinked rapidly several times. "What?"

"They've closed the road due to weather conditions."

"What do you mean?"

Troy raked a hand through his hair and blew out an uneasy breath. "The storm. It's bad. Emergency crews are closing roads everywhere along the front range."

Her eyes widened with the dawning. "I'm not going home?"

Troy shook his head while handing her his cell phone. "Not tonight."

She took the phone.

He grabbed a flashlight and headed upstairs to locate a pair of his sweatpants and thermal socks for her. He changed into a pair of thermal sweats himself before heading back downstairs. Laura handed him back the phone.

"Luke wants to talk to you."

Troy took the phone. "Hey, Luke. Uh-huh...really?" Smiling, he slanted Laura a glance. "She actually said that?"

"I said what? What's he telling you?" Laura stepped forward and reached out for the phone.

Troy brought his arm up, using his cast wrist to block her attempts at stealing the phone away while continuing his conversation with Luke. "Yeah, the power's really out. No, we're using candles. It's a gas fireplace. Romantic?" He laughed. "This is your aunt we're talking about. I'd rather take my chances with a wolverine."

Laura gasped and scrambled for the phone again. Troy playfully batted her hand away. "Hang on a second, Luke." Without moving his mouth away from the phone, he handed Laura the sweatpants and socks, and he winked. "Go put your pants on."

Her eyes grew wide with outrage. She ripped the articles of clothing out of his hand. "You don't have to say it like that!" She made another attempt to grab the receiver but Troy turned away.

"What's that, Luke? Yeah, she should be home sometime tomorrow afternoon. Do what?" He laughed. "We'll try, bye now." He ended the call, finally letting Laura snatch the phone away.

"We'll try what?" she demanded.

"Luke told us to have fun."

"*Put your pants on?* Why do you say things

like that?" She stomped her foot.

Troy looked down at her dainty little feet with their pink polished nails. His gaze moved up her legs. She stood, legs braced slightly apart with her hands planted on her hips. In one fist she held the cell phone, in the other, the pair of sweats and socks.

His gaze hop-skipped up the row of buttons on the front of her shirt, then back down to where the end of the hem dipped between her thighs. He felt chilled. He felt hot. Climbing the buttons back up to safety, his gaze clashed like flint against stone when he met hers, igniting a spark of fire in her green eyes.

Heaven help him, but she was the sexiest thing he'd ever seen.

"Ohhh, you're impossible!" Setting the phone on the counter, she headed for the kitchen door.

"Wait."

With her hand against the swinging door she stopped. "What now?"

"Take a candle or the flashlight with you. The house is dark, and if for nothing else it'll give you a sense of safety."

She glanced back over her shoulder and

raised an eyebrow. "And tell me, Troy, what more is there for me to fear in a dark room alone than what there is in a candlelit one with you?"

Troy picked up the flashlight and tucked it beneath his arm. "Suit yourself, princess. I was just trying to be helpful. All I'm saying is if you fall and hurt yourself, I'll take my time and be *very* thorough in checking for any broken bones and internal injuries." He flashed a smile. "And that, my dear, is a promise."

Laura dropped her hand from the door and marched back. "Oh, just shut-up and give me the blasted flashlight."

***

Two hours later, Troy pulled back the heavy living room drape and looked out through the swirling white of the blizzard's force. He was barely able to make out the high snowdrifts against the houses across the street.

"I called Luke again just to make sure things were still okay." Laura's voice came from behind him.

Troy turned, letting the drape fall back. "How's he doing? Everything okay?"

Amy Lynn

Laura walked through the dining room from the kitchen with her arms wrapped around her mid-section. "Great," she said. "Seems he's the lucky one. The electricity's still on at the house, so I'm sure it'll be a night of video games and microwave popcorn."

Electricity? Who needs it? If anything, Troy considered himself the lucky one tonight. After changing she'd come back down in a quieter mood. By candlelight they'd eaten dinner then sat and talked for sometime before she began gathering up the dishes.

When he'd told her they'd have to sleep in the living room with the fireplace, she agreed without protest. And though he tried not to appear too eager, he took the steps two at a time heading upstairs to gather blankets, quilts, and pillows.

Troy walked over and held his hand out to the gas-fed flames in the fireplace. He frowned. "There are a lot of people who wouldn't have done what you've done."

"What do you mean?"

"Taking on raising their nephew."

Laura shrugged. "His father, Jeff, was my brother. When Luke was nine, Jeff and Cathy were killed by a drunk driver. I petitioned the court for custody. I loved him. I couldn't stand the thought of not raising him myself."

"Yes, well if it means anything, from what I've seen, you've done one hell of a great job with the kid."

Laura laughed. "You wouldn't be saying that if you knew what my house was going to look like tomorrow after his night alone with the television and the refrigerator."

Troy smiled. "I remember those teenage years. Just be glad he isn't snowbound at the house with a girlfriend."

There was a moment of awkward silence before Laura turned away. "The cold's beginning to settle in."

Troy frowned, immediately sensing a sudden change in her mood. He could kick himself for mentioning the *being snowbound with a girl in the house* thing.

"I'm not sure the fire is going to warm very much past a few feet of the fireplace." Troy walked over to the leather sofa. "I'll take the couch. You can sleep on the floor close by the—"

"Whoa, wait a minute." Her expression was

one of disbelief. "No way."

"Fine, we'll flip a coin for the fireplace."

Laura laughed. "You've got to be kidding. Heads or tails, I'm taking the couch. After the cleaning I did in the kitchen today, I doubt I'd be able to move a muscle at all if I slept on the floor. Sorry cowboy, but you'll have to rough it tonight." She smiled, but he suspected it was falsely sympathetic.

"You're sure you want the couch?" He raised a brow.

"Why wouldn't I? Look." She pressed her hand down on the cushion several times before sitting on it to show its flexibility. "Almost like a Beauty Rest mattress, if I might say so myself."

Next she stood and moved to a spot in front of the softly flickering fire. Squatting, she pressed her hand into the thick carpet. "Mmmm, feels to me like the ground. I imagine a cowboy accustomed to sleeping out in the open and wishing on falling stars would prefer it, wouldn't you say?"

Troy suppressed a smile at her demonstration. Silently he agreed the *cowboy wishing on stars* comment was a nice touch.

Her bright smile and happy face reminded

him of a kid, thinking they'd found the best seat in a crowded movie theatre. Hell, why spoil the moment for her. She'd find out soon enough. Still, he had to ask once more. "Are you sure you want the couch?"

"Positive." She flipped a thick strand of hair over her shoulder and pointed her nose in the air. "Now quit repeating yourself like a parrot and leave me alone. And by the way, you can fix your own bed. I've already done it once today, and I'm not doing it again until next week."

"Just want to make sure. I wouldn't want you to get yourself into something you'll end up regretting in the morning."

That caused a spark!

Her mouth pressed into a thin line and her eyes narrowed. "What's that remark supposed to mean?"

Troy shrugged. "Nothing. If you insist on the couch, far be it from me not to be a gentleman and let you have it. I only wanted to make sure it's what you wanted. Just seeing to your needs, you might say."

"Liar. That comment wasn't about the couch."

Troy dropped a blanket on the floor at his feet where he would sleep. He faced her. "Okay, princess, then let's just discuss what you think it *is* about."

Laura froze then swallowed hard. She watched him stand there, tall, lean and handsome. The perfect romantic backdrop of the fireplace behind him clashed with his challenge for her to discuss why she regretted sleeping with him.

She cocked her chin. "Just don't you worry. I won't regret the choice. In fact, I'd say you sleeping on the floor is just desserts for the mess you left in the kitchen." That said, she settled herself on the couch and gave the top blanket a good shake until it floated down to cover her. She folded her arms beneath her head, and with what she hoped was her best imitation of a Cheshire grin, sighed with blissful exaggeration and shut her eyes, leaving him to lay out his own bedding.

***

Hours later, Laura lay on her side, her head buried deep beneath the covers. She drew her knees up against her chest, trying desperately to hold onto any heat that had not managed to escape through the micro pores of the blanket. She was a shivering bundle of regret.

Barely able to move her cold-stiffened fingers, she inched the blanket off her head to steal a glance at Troy some distance away. He lay on his back, shirtless. His blanket was pushed to his waist and his cast wrist rest over his abdomen. Laura watched the steady rise and fall of his chest.

She tried to pace her breathing with his, but with each exhale, her teeth chattered together like a pair of wind up dime store dentures.

He looked warm. Too warm. Dang near toasty, in fact. The nerve of the man!

"T-T-Troy?"

He didn't stir.

"Troy!" She managed a louder whisper through her clenched teeth. He moved, rolling over and turning his back to her.

"T-T-Troy!" She chattered louder this time, sounding more like a Morse code message.

"Hmmm?" came his sleepy reply.

"T-Troy?"

"What?"

"I'm c-cold." It was a humiliating confession.

"Do you want another blanket?"

"N-n-no. No b-blankets." Her slight frame was racked with another bout of shivers.

"Then what is it you want from me?"

"T-trade p-places." She wanted to add *please* but feared the word would come out sounding like the sputtering of a plane engine nose diving to the ground.

He said nothing, didn't move, giving her to wonder if he'd fallen back to sleep. "T-Troy, are y-you awake?"

"I heard you."

"Well?"

"I'm thinking, Laura," he drawled. "I don't know many cowboys who'd trade the hard ground for the comfort of a Beauty Rest mattress."

"I'm s-s-sorry I said t-that." Though right now she'd apologize for the sins of her grandmother if it meant a chance to get warm.

"Apology accepted."

Laura shivered and waited for him to continue, for him to be a gentleman and tell her he'd trade places and let her sleep by the fire, but he didn't say a word.

"W-well? Are you going to t-trade me?"

"No."

Taken aback, Laura stared at the back of his

handsome head. She tried again, inflecting a little groveling into her voice for good measure. "I'm freezing t-to death, p-p-please, let me sleep by the f-fire."

Troy rolled over. He lifted the corner of the blanket, and Laura's heart took a sudden leap for joy. Almost afraid a smile would crack her frozen face, she tried to convey her appreciation through her eyes. She tossed off her own covering. A blast of colder air greeted her, but she didn't care. She was going to sleep on the floor, next to the fireplace!

Her joyfully beating heart slowed when she noticed, though still holding up the corner of the blanket, he'd not moved in the direction of the couch. "W-what are you d-doing?"

"Rolling over. The heat's getting to be a little too much, but you're more than welcome to join me if you want."

"B-b-but…" she spewed and stuttered like a lawn mower with a choked up carburetor.

"You risk more chance of exposure up there alone than you would down here with me. I give you my word."

"Your word?"

"My word."

Before the voice of doubt settled in, Laura sprang to her feet and settled in beside him.

CHAPTER FOURTEEN

TROY LAY on his side behind Laura. He gritted his teeth, swearing silently for the thousandth time as she brushed her soft backside against his loins. With his ample supply of willpower dwindling at an alarming rate, he forced himself to lay still, praying her restlessness would soon cease.

Seconds of stillness crawled by until he felt able to quietly exhale the breath he'd been holding. Slowly, tension eased from his body. Maybe now he could concentrate on getting to sleep.

Laura wiggled.

Troy sucked in a sharp breath and squeezed his eyes together tightly. A burst of stars filled the darkness behind his lids. He gritted his teeth, trying to focus on one. *One more wish. Just give me one more wish!*

Again she wiggled, brushing against his swelling erection. He placed his cast hand firmly on her hip and growled. "Quit moving."

"I'm sorry," Laura whispered back. "I'm just trying to get comfortable."

"Well, it's making me very damned uncomfortable!"

Her squirming stopped instantly. Her apology was barely audible. "Sorry."

He smiled.

He never should have offered to share the floor. He should have just been a gentleman and traded places. His victory at having her on the floor with him had been short-lived.

Laura wiggled.

He huffed.

"I'm sorry," she said. "It's the floor. It's too hard."

Oh honey, I could show you hard. Troy clamped his teeth together.

Once more she moved.

That did it. He threw off the blanket. What he needed was a cold shower, or better still, a good butt-naked dive into a snowdrift.

Laura glanced over her shoulder. "Where are you going?"

He pinned her with a frustrated glare. Her wide-eyed expression appeared innocent, trusting.

Keeper of the Stars

Yet he knew staying beside her any longer would have him doing something that would wind up getting him slapped.

"I'm going to sleep on the couch."

"But it's freezing up there."

"Good!"

"Don't go," Laura entreated softly. The request tore at his heart. "I'll quit moving, I promise." She bunched the pillow up under her head then lay very still. "How's this?"

Troy dropped to the couch, resting his elbows on his knees. He bent his head between his hands and raked his fingers through his hair.

If he were to lay back down beside her, there was the chance they would make love again, and he knew it was too soon for her. Still, if she were to get a good night's sleep, she would need the added warmth of his body to do so.

He glanced up to find her watching him expectantly. "I don't know, Laura."

"Please, it's your body warmth that makes the difference," she added as if able to read his mind.

Ah, hell! What could he say to that? No?

Wearily he stood, feeling as though he'd

just come through one battle and was headed into another without a chance to recoup.

Laura scooted over. She pulled the covers back for him to lie in front of her this time. Once settled in, she moved close but made no contact. For several long minutes, Troy lay in uncertain silence.

"Goodnight, Troy." Her voice was a sleepy whisper behind his ear.

He waited several moments for sleep to take her before responding. "Goodnight, princess."

"Mmmm." Laura sighed in her sleep, pressing herself against him.

His breath caught as her breasts burned their impression into his back. Finally settled, she lay still, falling deeper into the world of dreams and fantasies. Reaching behind him he brought her arm around and held it against his chest. Finally, he felt able to close his eyes.

***

The sound of soft whimpering woke him.

"Noooo." From behind him the moaning came again. Deep in sleep, Laura stirred fitfully, pulling her hand from his.

"Nooo, don't." She thrashed her legs about under the covers.

Troubled by the unknown cause of her restlessness, Troy sat up and turned around. The fear filling her voice pulled his protective instincts to the surface.

She stirred fitfully.

"Laura?" He smoothed the hair from her dampened brow, trying gently to wake her.

"D-don't touch me." Her hand came up and pushed his away.

Troy tried gently shaking her shoulder. "Laura."

"Please, no more." Her head rolled from side to side. She whimpered then thrashed about again. "Ohhh, Troy, please help me." She drew a knee up, kicking off the covers. "Where are you?"

"Wake up, Laura, I'm here."

Instead, she struggled against his touch, becoming entangled in her unbound hair. The restriction caused her to fight harder.

With more insistence, he called her name, fighting against the urge to restrain her flailing hands.

"Don't hurt me," she sobbed. "Please,

Steve, don't..."

As she cried out in tortured anguish, Troy watched a tear make a glistening trail from the corner of her eye into her hair at her temple. Feeling the burn of tears behind his own eyes, he cursed his inability to help her.

Though he had his suspicions, the truth to his questions was a blow to his mind, wrenching his heart. Steve had been the cause of her scars, both inside and out. Steve was the hell she had been through.

Troy gathered her up against his chest, making sure he didn't restrain her arms. "Sssshhh," he soothed into her ear, rocking her slowly back and forth. He stroked the back of her hair and rubbed his cheek against its soft thickness near her ear. "I'm here, Laura. I'm here. Come on back to me, sweetheart."

He felt her body suddenly tense, and knew. She had awakened. She threw her arms around his neck and buried her face against his shoulder. She sobbed uncontrollably.

Troy held her. He asked no questions, only filling her ear with words of love and reassurance.

"He hurt me, Troy. He'd hit me, then...then he'd—"

"I know, baby, I know." He dragged in a ragged breath, understanding the words she couldn't say. "But he's gone now and can't ever hurt you again. Not ever again."

She pulled back, and with a tortured gaze, touched a finger to her temple. "But he's in here, Troy. He's in here, and he won't go away. Please," she choked, "please make him go away."

Troy gathered her against his chest and squeezed his eyes shut. "I've been trying, honey. God knows, I've been trying."

What else could he tell her? He knew he loved her. He knew there was nothing he wouldn't do for her. He knew there was no distance he wouldn't go for her, and yet, he *didn't* know how to make Steve's memory go away.

***

Slowly Laura awoke from exhausted sleep. She stretched on her side and winced at the muscle cramp in her lower back. Her hand brushed the spot in front of her, but found it empty. She opened her eyes. Troy was gone.

She snuggled deeper beneath her blanket and gathered her thoughts.

Troy knew.

While he'd held her in his arms last night, she'd told him everything about Steve. He asked little and said even less. She'd sensed his wanting to help but his uncertainty of what to do. He'd told her again he loved her, asking her once more to marry him.

She smiled. She felt different this morning, as if her confession to Troy had exercised Steve's voice from her head.

Bunching the pillow under her head, she sighed. The lamp on the end table glowed dimly. Electricity was restored. Sunlight cut through the gap where the drapes were pulled together. She wondered about the time.

Yawning, she pushed off the blanket. Perhaps the roads had been cleared and Troy had left to see his father at the hospital, leaving her to sleep. She smiled at his thoughtfulness. Still, she needed to dress and get home.

Without another thought, Laura rose and began folding the bedding she and Troy had slept on. With her arms loaded with blankets, she headed for the upstairs linen closet.

Passing by the dining room entrance, she smelled freshly cooked bacon and eggs. The odor hit her nostrils, pitching her stomach into a somersault. She managed to control the sudden gagging reflex and glanced around. Too late. Dropping the blankets where she stood, she made a mad dash for the bathroom.

She made it just in time to lift the toilet seat and pull her hair out of the way before her body was racked with violent, uncontrollable spasms.

With one last shudder she finished then flushed the commode. Pulling a washcloth from the cabinet she wet it and pressed it against her face. She let a few moment pass before she glanced up to study her reflection in the mirror. Though her face appeared pale, she felt much better, as if the vomiting had cured the cause. But she knew it hadn't.

Laura placed her hand over her lower abdomen. This, Troy still didn't know about. Telling him of her pregnancy on top of the other confession? Could he have handled so much information?

'Poor little, Laura. A pregnant whore. What a predicament you're in. If you're not sure what to do then just answer this, what would I have done to you if you'd told me you were pregnant? He's a man, Laura.

Amy Lynn

No knight in shining armor.'

Steve's accusations and threats echoed through her mind. He was still there. She gripped the edge of the sink and hung her head. The sound she pushed from her throat was half laugh, half sob.

"Laura, are you okay?"

Laura whirled around to find Troy standing in the bathroom doorway. He was dressed in a pair of Wranglers and black short sleeved tee-shirt, his face smoothly shaven.

Her heart swelled with emotion. Here stood the most handsome and caring man she'd ever met. Hers for the taking if she wanted.

"I-I thought you were gone," she lied, stammering, struggling terribly for composure, not thinking quickly enough for anything more believable to say.

His expression became unreadable, yet she had no doubt that he was thinking something. And that became the one thing she had to keep him from doing. He had proven himself too perceptive where she was concerned.

"Has it stopped snowing? Are the roads clear?" She was rambling, talking too fast. She knew it.

"The storm is over." His answer came on the heels of an uncomfortable hesitation as though snow was the last thing he had on his mind. "I fixed breakfast. Are you hungry?"

Eat food? I can't even stand to smell it. Still, she managed to hide her panic behind a mask of cheerfulness. "Oh God, I'm absolutely famished. Give me a few minutes to freshen up and I'll be right out."

"Sure." He turned but not before he threw a glance at the toilet with the raised seat, then back at her. He raised a brow. "You feeling well?"

"Of course." She forced a smile, waving her hand in a dismissing gesture. "I'll be out in a few moments."

Troy stepped out. At the soft click of the closing door, all strength left her body and she slowly slid down the wall and collapsed to the floor in despair. "God help me, what am I doing?" she murmured.

If she did manage to eat breakfast, how on earth was she going to be able to keep it down? He would know something was wrong. He'd ask questions. She couldn't tell him. Not yet. Not until she had time to think. Right now she just wanted to go home.

Laura hugged her arms around drawn-up knees, trying desperately to come up with an answer to her dilemma.

He'd offered marriage. She wiped away a tear. She couldn't go to him with the kind of emotional baggage she carried with her. Steve's voice in her head and Troy's baby in her womb.

Troy wouldn't understand her reasoning. He would argue with her about it, she knew that. But she needed to make him see there was no future for them until she settled her past. However she was going to do that. One night of lying in his arms talking about the abuse hadn't erased the years of nightmares.

Before a plan could formulate itself in her head, the bathroom door swung open. Panicked, she looked up.

"How long have you known?" Troy demanded.

Laura opened her mouth then closed it. Her heart slammed against the inside of her chest as if seeking a means of escape. Her throat went dry. She swallowed hard. "I-I don't know what you're talking about." At least she hoped she didn't. Still, he seemed too sure of his question.

"Don't play me for a fool, Laura." Anger edged his tone. Or was it hurt?

She dropped her chin to her knees, focusing her gaze on the floor. She released a ragged sigh. "I found out for sure last week."

She heard him move away from the doorway. A second later the toes of his boots came into view. She ran her gaze up the length of his creased pant leg but didn't have to go much farther, for he knelt and looked her in the eye. He rested his cast wrist over his bent knee.

"A week ago? When were you going to tell me?" His voice carried a mixed array of emotions, none she dared try to pinpoint.

She searched the shimmering gray steel of his eyes and shrugged. "I-I don't know, Troy. I suppose I would've told you eventually."

"When?" he demanded sharply. "When you couldn't hide the fact from me anymore?"

"You'd have been back in Montana by then." The words were out before she could stop them.

He swore beneath his breath.

She lowered her gaze.

"Why the hell didn't you tell me before I

made you clean the house yesterday?" He swore beneath his breath again. "The mess I left the kitchen...were you hoping something would happen and you'd lose the baby?"

"No!" she gasped, covering her abdomen with a protective hand. "God, no."

"Then..." his tone gentled. "You want this baby?"

"More than anything."

She thought the confession would make him happy but instead another wave of darkness clouded his expression, blowing over her like a cold northern, chilling her to the bone. "You want our baby, but you don't want me?"

His question left her speechless. Laura blinked and glanced away. *Now's the time to tell him. Now, before he tried to talk her into walking through life with him while she still lugged around so much of her past.*

"I'm afraid."

Troy slowly reached out and cupped her cheek, his voice heartbreakingly gentle. "I'm not your ex-husband, Laura. Give me a chance."

It's a chance I'm not sure my heart can take right now. How many nights of love could they share before the nightmares came again? How many smiles and moments of laughter would she be able to give him before a gesture or tone triggered memories of Steve's abuse? What kind of life would that be for him, never knowing when the moments of remembering would come? Like in a fairytale, their love seemed cursed.

Laura's vision blurred. A tear rolled down her cheek. She closed her eyes against the gentle plea in his eyes. Turning her face into his hand, she pressed her lips, soft and lingering against his palm. She breathed in. His scent filled her head, calling out to her heart. She sighed, absently grateful his cologne didn't have the same effect on her as his cooking.

His hand felt strong and callused used to hard work and heavy lifting. But his hands wouldn't have to carry her burden, his heart would.

"I need time, Troy."

He released her cheek and brushed his hand through the side of her hair. His breath gently touched her face. "You don't have much time, sweetheart."

Laura looked into his eyes, shaking her head slowly. "If it's an answer you want this very minute, then I'm saying no."

Laura was unprepared for the measure of pain that surfaced in his eyes. Her own anguish bordered on a physical pain. He dropped his hand, taking the warmth of his touch away. He stood. Laura looked up.

"What is it you need time for, Laura?" he asked. "For your knight in shining armor to come riding up, declare his love and take you away? Do you think the nightmares will end then?"

"I-I don't know." She shrugged. "Maybe." *It's what I wished for.*

Tense silence filled the following moments, stretching like a rubber band, snapping back with Troy's exhale and pulling with it the weight of the world. He spread his arms. "Then open your eyes, Laura, and take a good look at me. We don't wear armor anymore. We dress just like everybody else." And with that, he turned and walked out.

CHAPTER FIFTEEN

"WELL, REBEL, what do you think?" Troy questioned, arching a brow. He held his arms wide while Scott buckled the last leather strap of the breastplate.

Rebecca stifled a cry.

"That's a good sign, right?" Troy glanced beneath his arm at Scott.

Scott peered over Troy's shoulder toward Rebecca. He shook his head, returning his attention to the task at hand. "I think its Cupid's cry of happiness." He ran his finger between the material of Troy's shirt and the leather strap, making sure he hadn't buckled him in too tightly.

"You..." Rebecca sniffed. "You look just like a real knight in shining armor." She turned him toward the full-length mirror. Their glances met in the reflection.

Troy smiled wryly. "I hope this works."

"It will," Rebecca said before reaching in her pocket, extracting a tissue to wipe a tear from her eye. "It's just *so* romantic."

Scott gave Troy a hearty slap on the shoulder, the metal armor clanking loudly. "You know you've ruined it for the rest of the bachelor population, don't you?"

"How's that?" Troy asked, giving his image in the full body suit of armor a critical study.

"After getting a look at you and what you're willing to do to win a lady's heart, no woman will ever be satisfied with a box of chocolates and a dozen roses again."

Troy worked his arm back and forth, testing his ease of movement. He expelled an expressive breath. "Man, for the first time in my life I'm scared to death about what a woman wants."

"Welcome to the real world of love, bro." Scott gave Troy another slap on the back. The force of the hit carried Troy a step forward, almost upsetting his balance.

Troy reached for his gauntlets. "Is Comanche loaded in the trailer?"

He'd spent the last three days driving to Montana, loading up his favorite horse, and driving back to Colorado in order to be back by Valentine's Day. A race against time, but he'd done it. The suit of armor he'd borrowed from an old college buddy who worked in the wardrobe department of a production company. Troy was grateful the mock suit was lighter than the authentic ones.

"Comanche's ready," Scott replied.

Troy glanced at Rebecca. "Did you call Donna to make sure she keeps Laura at the house?"

"Taken care of." Rebecca smiled through her tears.

Troy placed a knuckle under her chin, tipping her head up to meet his gaze. "I thought it was a crazy idea when you first asked me to rescue Laura. But now..." he placed a brotherly peck on her forehead and whispered, "...let's hope Cupid's arrow hit true."

The door to the room burst open and in bounded Brandon, his seven-year-old nephew. The boy stopped in his tracks and looked wide-eyed at the armor. "Wow! That's cool! Can I wear one of those too, Uncle Troy?"

To the sound of gently clanking metal and creaking leather, Troy bent to one knee before the boy. Mentally, he breathed a sigh of relief knowing he could kneel if he had to.

With a sober expression, he looked his nephew directly in the eye. "First, you have to fall in love with a girl."

Brandon made a face. "With a *girl*?"

Troy nodded solemnly. "With a girl."

Brandon scrunched his nose. "I won't have to kiss her, will I?"

"Oh yeah." Troy smiled. "That's one of the prizes you win."

"Yuck! That's no prize. I'd rather kiss a frog."

Laughing, Troy ruffled Brandon's hair. "Please, one fairytale at a time." Standing, he glanced at Scott and Rebecca, and then gave a slight nod. "Ready?"

***

"I don't want to stand outside on the balcony," Laura stated, even as she followed Donna up the stairs, working to keep her cup of decaf coffee from sloshing over the rim and onto her hand.

"But it would do you some good. I believe I read somewhere that pregnant women have hot flashes."

"I don't think that happens until later."

"Well, you could get them now, right?

"I suppose I could, but I'm not."

Donna reached the second floor and turned around. Her eyes lit up. "Then we'll stand out on the balcony and soak in the beauty of the day."

"The only thing we're likely to get is pneumonia. It's February, Donna." Valentine's Day. "It's freezing outside. How about we soak up the beauty looking out from the inside?"

"But—"

"No."

"I read somewhere pregnant women are supposed to get lots of fresh air."

"You read too much."

Donna walked to the balcony door and looked out. "Just for a few minutes?"

"No."

"You're no fun," Donna grumbled.

Laura set her cup on the dresser and threw her hands up. "For crying out loud, Donna. Talking to you is like talking to Troy."

Donna whirled around. "Okay, since we're talking about Troy, how is that handsome devil doing anyway?"

Laura turned away. "We weren't talking about Troy." But the unexpected mention of his name stirred awake the butterflies in her stomach. She moved to the bed, fluffing pillows, for something distracting to do. She masked the dejection she felt from her voice. "I haven't seen nor heard from him since the morning he found out I was pregnant."

Perhaps her rejection of his marriage proposal had been the reason. She just needed some time. Angrily, Laura swiped a hand across a small crease in the comforter on her bed. *Damn him anyway!* He knew her better than she knew herself. Why did he choose that time, of all times, to believe her? Still, what was said was said and what was done was done

"He does really love you, you know," Donna said softly.

Laura threw a glaring glance over her shoulder. "I don't remember waking this morning to find him on my doorstep with an arm full of roses and chocolates."

"Chocolates, *schmocklates*. What about the baby? That little miracle is going to need a father."

"I need a good man first."

"I could still hook you up with someone

from Scott's office."

"Oh heavens no!" Laura choked out.

"Why not? They're nice guys."

"Because...because," Laura stammered.

"Because you're in love with Troy."

"I never said that."

"I don't think you've ever said it."

Laura felt backed into a corner.

Donna smiled. "You seem to have lost your coloring. I read somewhere that fresh air will put the color back in your cheeks." She opened the balcony door and grabbed Laura's arm.

Laura allowed herself to be pulled along, grudgingly admitting to herself, the cold air actually did feel good. She felt invigorated by its coolness in her lungs.

Gazing out from the balcony, she and Donna settled into a comfortable silence. Laura couldn't talk. She was too busy thinking.

How could she deny it? She did love Troy. Not a night had passed since they'd made love that she didn't yearn to feel his arms about her, his whispers of tenderness in her ear, or the scent of his cologne seducing her senses. If he ever gave her the chance again, she would tell him.

"So," Donna ended the silence. "Tell me about this falling star you wished on."

"Rebecca needs to mind her own business."

"Well, I think it's romantic." Donna turned and leaned back against the balcony railing. "Did your wish come true?"

Laura gave her hand a flittering gesture, her tone sarcastic. "Do you *see* a knight in shining armor?"

Donna glanced at her watch. "Not yet."

Feeling an unexplained restlessness, Laura pushed away from the balcony railing. "I'm cold. I'm going in."

"Wait!"

"For what?" Laura exhaled impatiently. "What's wrong with you? You've been acting goofy all morning."

"Nothing's wrong."

Laura opened her mouth to argue but shut it again. She looked out across her lawn. An unfamiliar sound carried through the air.

Sitting tall in the saddle, a knight in full armor approached from the street to her right. Atop his helmet, a large red feathered plume waved in the breeze. The face guard hid his identity.

But it didn't matter, she knew him. She knew him from her dreams, she knew him from a night of passion. She knew him from wishing on a falling star.

A sudden, unexpected break in the overcast clouds sent down a ray of sunlight. Like a spotlight upon the approaching knight, it reflected off the armor.

The horse stepped high. Draped over the horse's flanks flowed a blanket of red, embroidered with the emblem of a black hawk. The sight rendered Laura speechless.

She placed a trembling hand against her throat. Oh yes, this was so much better than chocolates.

Several of her neighbors stepped from their homes and followed some distance behind the knight. The small assembly stopped short of the sidewalk in front of her house, but the horse and rider continued on.

The great steed carefully picked its way across her front lawn, stopping just below the balcony. The knight raised his head to her. Settled in the shadows, behind the vertical slits of his helmet, Laura caught his gaze.

Amy Lynn

Gray steel, strong and unyielding, watched her. His look so intense it stole her breath. He turned his attention from her for a moment and nodded.

Laura glanced at Donna, the recipient of the nod.

"Later, love." Donna smiled, rolling her fingers in a departing gesture before she turned and walked back into the house.

Staring blankly at the closed French door, Laura realized she was on her own. She glanced back to the knight below.

Troy swore quietly under his breath. He was as nervous as hell. His palms had become uncomfortably sweaty inside the leather gloves. He'd given up hope of ever having a normal heartbeat again.

Laura had never looked more beautiful to him. As he watched her reaction he remained uncertain whether it was a sign of happiness or tortured embarrassment at this latest attempt to sway her heart. Through the slits of his helmet he focused on her eyes, praying for a glimmer of hope. Her eyes shone with the glimmer of unshed tears.

He pushed back the face shield, nervously

clearing his throat. "My lady," he began. "Once you wished upon a star, for a knight in shining armor. Is there a word of hope you can give me that your wish has come true? Might I be the one?"

Laura brushed away a tear. Though her smile appeared shaky, it changed the beat of his heart from one of total nervousness to the hope he sought.

"If a true knight in shining armor you be, then tell me how you'll rescue me."

Each breath Troy took in came a little easier, as it appeared she would play the game with him. "I have heard tales of old, of a time when men braved the fiercest enemy in the darkest realm to keep their true love safe and protected."

"Am-am I your true love?"

Troy touched a gauntlet covered hand gently to a spot over his chest. "Aye, my lady, for my heart has declared it to be so."

"But it is my heart, tightly gripped in the dragon's talons," she said, placing a hand over her own heart. "How would you free me?"

Not until this moment did Troy realize just

how much she needed this. He loved her and wanted so much to hold her and protect her. But first there was the small matter of slaying a certain dragon. And regardless of the outcome, he was going to play this moment out for all she had dreamed or wished it to be.

"Aye, and though I am here to battle an enemy I cannot see, a dragon so fierce no lance or sword has yet been welded that can pierce its flesh, I believe I have found a weapon that can."

He watched a smile tug at the corners of Laura's mouth. "Then do not wait a moment longer, use it and destroy this hellish creature that torments my sleep and thoughts."

Troy pulled the helmet from his head, settling it in the crook of his arm. He furrowed his brow. "Alas, my lady, it can only be destroyed when this weapon is used by the two of us together."

"And where is this weapon?"

Comanche shifted restlessly beneath Troy. The gentle clink of armor echoed in the crisp afternoon air. "Within your own heart there is a door. Though I am here and will fight to protect you, only you have the means to let me in. You have the key."

Keeper of the Stars

"I once dreamed a dream," Laura began quietly. "In a sleep so deep and a dungeon so dark there seemed no hope that I would be found. Then you came…"

The anguish in her voice tightened an emotional band around his chest. Pain tore through him as if the razor sharp talons of a real dragon had pierced him through.

He watched a tear roll down her cheek, unable to wipe it away. His gaze followed its path until it fell free from her delicate chin, descending to the earth below. On impulse he leaned forward in his saddle and reached out his gloved hand.

The teardrop hit the center of his leathered palm. His gaze lingered on its dampness before he gently closed it within his fist. He glanced up. "Only you have the key to the door. Please, Laura, let me in."

What could he say to her that he had not already said to make her see he could shoulder her pain and love away her fears?

"I-I don't know where it is, Troy." She brushed away another tear.

Troy curled his fingers around her tear and touched his fist to his chest. "Here, in your heart."

Amy Lynn

You've never said you love me, Laura. Say it now, baby. Torn, he watched several more tears fall from her sea-green eyes.

"It's been so long since I've seen the key. Please tell me what it looks like. I'll let you in, if you just tell me what it looks like."

From somewhere in the small crowd behind him came the sound of sniffling, but Troy ignored the distraction, staying focused on the battle he was fighting before him. "I cannot tell you, Laura. You have to find the key on your own. Just close your eyes and let your heart show you. Please try. I cannot come in and fight the dragon until you find the key."

In her expression Troy read the signs of one who bore too many bad memories and the fear of trusting even more. Helplessly, he watched her struggle.

Laura closed her eyes and saw Steve. Standing guard at the gate refusing to set her free. She shook her head against his intruding voice. *'Bitch, whore, worthless little lying slut. You're mine, Laura. 'Til death do us part, remember, baby. Do you think he'll put up with you like I did? When he finds out it's because of you Bobby died.'*

The sharp talons of the dragon pierced her

soul, pushing deeper the guilt of Bobby's death until it threatened to consume her. And Laura knew the wounds would never heal nor the shadow of guilt ever leave her, no matter how much love Troy gave her.

With a heart on the verge of dying she knew there was but one answer she could give this loving knight who had tried so hard to win her heart and give his all to be her hero.

"Troy..." she began as the growing lump of pain in her throat threatened to suffocate her before she could finish. "Troy, darling...I-I can't." The flood gate gave way and her tears spilled over. She squeezed her eyes shut and took a ragged breath. Oh dear God, she needed to find the strength to finish this.

'Finish what, Laura?' From within came the softest of whispers. Different from the dragon. Her heart clutched. It was Bobby. He would never have wanted her to live with the guilt of his death. He would have wanted to her to be happy. Bobby was the key.

In the space of a moment, the memories came flooding back and she found herself facing the dragon, armed only with her love for Troy, and the dragon with the guilt of Bobby's death.

She knew what she was seeing wasn't real, but it was her mind's way of settling the past. Telling her the journey she had been on all these years was ending.

Bobby always gave her strength in her times of weakness.

From behind her came the slightest of whispers. A breeze? A sigh? *'My death was not your fault, Laura. The dragon's weapon is powerless. You are free to love again.'*

Opening her eyes, she turned to the French doors and hopelessly blinked through the blur of tears.

Below the balcony, Troy sat speechless.

The reaction of the gathering behind him went from a shocked gasp to a deathly quiet. Troy found no words to describe the blow to his heart at hearing the door above him shut. For several moments he sat stunned, paralyzed in disbelief. Finally he swallowed a deep, burning painful breath then squared his shoulders beneath the armor.

He'd gambled. And he'd lost.

The reins weighed heavy in his hand as he lifted them and turned Comanche around. The soft *clink* and *clank* of his armor sounding more like a death toll of a failed rescue. A sudden gust of wind pushed through the high branches of the leafless trees, wailing and moaning as if the whole of creation mourned the dying of his heart on this Valentine's Day.

Comanche's hooves struck hard against the cold February ground. Troy worked him back across the lawn and over the sidewalk. The crowd silently parted to let him pass.

Though the sound of a door opening was faint, it was as loud as cannon fire in his mind. He reined Comanche to a halt. Beneath the shining armor his heart beat wildly. He held his breath. Dare he turn around? What if it wasn't—?

"I love you!"

Troy squeezed his eyes shut. Her spoken words released the breath he'd held deep in his lungs.

"I love you, my knight in shining armor," Laura called out again.

He turned and looked back.

She stood in her doorway.

Troy turned Comanche and worked his way back to her. Laura left the porch and ran to meet him. When she was beside him, he removed his glove and reached down. He tenderly cupped her cheek in his palm, allowing his gaze to sweep over her face. Finally his gaze settled on her eyes. He kept his voice low and steady. "You have found the key. Love. Now tell me, did your wish come true?"

"Yes." She rubbed her cheek against his hand. The look in her eyes filled him with wonder. "More than I could have ever imagined. I love you, Troy.

"And I love you, princess."

Leaning down, he wrapped his arm around her waist and scooped her up and into his lap. He looked into her eyes. "I've always wondered, what exactly it was you wished for the night we saw that falling star."

Laura looked at the man before her, dressed in knight's armor. She recalled his persistence in melting away the wall of ice around her heart. And she remembered the spark of love he had set within the depth of her heart. A night when he had stoked that spark into a raging fire of passion. Wild emotion surged up within her again.

"It's actually a rhyme my grandmother taught me when I was a little girl. Maker, keeper of the stars, release for me one wishing star, followed by a trail of light to shine upon my hearts delight. A love to come and right the wrong, a knight in shining armor strong."

"Wishes do come true then." Troy leaned forward to kiss her but was interrupted.

"It took you long enough to get here. I was beginning to worry," Donna said, making her way up the walk from the house.

Troy gave her a half smile then pitched the helmet to her. "I had my problems. It's not easy getting into one of these contraptions. But it was definitely worth it." He turned his head and looked into Laura's eyes. Knowing he'd been patient long enough in waiting to sample another one of her kisses, he closed the distance between them.

A short time later, after the neighbors had gone back to their homes with a story they would be telling their great-grandchildren, Laura sidled up to Troy as he was loading Comanche into the trailer. She pressed against him. "Troy?"

He glanced down and watched her fingers trail across the breastplate of his armor. Her smile filled his heart with warmth and his body with desire. He arched a black eyebrow in question. "Yes, my lady?"

"How soon do you have to return the suit of armor to the rental shop?"

Troy cocked a smile to one side. His arm circled her waist. He drew her tighter against him and felt himself grow hard at her seductive attention. "I didn't rent it; I borrowed it from a friend. Why?" His smile grew suspiciously wider. "Are you trying to tell me you suddenly have a thing for a man in uniform?"

"Well, as a matter of fact," she began as her sweet scent rose up to fill his head and her softness triggered sweeter memories. "I've always had this fantasy..."

About the Author

Alaska born Amy Lynn grew up the middle child in a military family. As a "military brat" she experienced a life of changes and travel: from Alaska to Florida to Germany (twice), North Carolina, and a few more temporary homes in between. Two weeks after her high school graduation, she settled in Denver, Colorado.

Amy is married with three children, 4 grandchildren, 3 Chihuahua's and one cat named Busy. An artist and a writer, Amy won several awards for her pictures, paintings, and sculptures. She also won 2nd Place in Colorado's Heart of the Rockies Contest for her debut book, "Keeper of the Stars."

When not working her full time job, Amy enjoys reading, drawing, writing romantic fiction and poetry, wood carving, and shooting her compound bow.

Find more great short stories and novels at

www.twbpress.com

www.twbpress.com/amoremoonpublishing